Eleanor, Elizabeth

Eleanor, Elizabeth

Libby Gleeson

HOLIDAY HOUSE / NEW YORK

Copyright © Libby Gleeson 1984
Originally published in Australia by Angus & Robertson Publishers
First American publication 1990 by Holiday House, Inc.
Printed in the United States of America

Library of Congress Cataloging-in-Publication Data

Gleeson, Libby.
  Eleanor, Elizabeth / written by Libby Gleeson.
     p.   cm.
  Summary: Having left the town and the friends of her childhood, a
twelve-year-old Australian girl finds the land and the house of her
grandmother to be an alien place, full of other people's memories.
  ISBN 0-8234-0804-3
  [1. Australia—Fiction. 2. Grandmothers—Fiction.] I. Title.
PZ7.G48148E1   1990   89-36009   CIP   AC
[Fic]—dc20

For Gwynneth, Josie and Alice;
mothers and grandmothers

"*I* spy with my little eye something beginning with B."

"Bush."

"No."

"Ben Lomond."

"No." Ken glanced out the side window of the car and then back at his younger sister. "You can't still see that."

Eleanor knelt on the back seat and her green eyes squinted. Her freckled nose banged against the back glass as they swung round a bend. "Well you could a minute ago. When we started." She fell back into the corner, rubbed her nose and tucked her pale, thin legs underneath her.

Ken pulled a frayed thread from his shorts. His legs were longer now than hers. "Anyway, it's not. D'you give in?"

"Not yet." She slid forward so her feet rested on the floor by her thongs and Billy's sandals. The wind blew her short red hair into her eyes. She flicked her fringe back. "I know. It's Bill."

"No way. Too easy."

Billy lay curled up between them, damp brown curls on his forehead. His cheek made a wet patch on the seat. He'd been asleep since the pink morning drive through the still town. The car windows had been white with their breath. She'd written her name with one finger on the cold, misty glass.

"Box of Minties."

"No. I've gotcha now, El." Ken laughed at her.

She knelt on the seat and rested her arms on the window ledge. It was fat green country. Black and white cows peered over tidy fences. The roads were winding, familiar. Across the Tableland and down. Down the mountain. Down from New England. Holiday roads, hairpin and gorge. Past the farms and down. Down potholes and boulders to the cottages, freckles and the salt-tasting sand.

B for burn and B for blister. B for Brunswick Heads. But not this time. No wet swimmers, fish and chips for tea. No home, back up the mountain, past Grafton and Tenterfield, high in the crisp, cool air. Not this time.

West. Out West. You'll burn up out West. It's a hundred in the shade. Earth's red, rivers are slow. Flat as a board. B for board. Go West young man. Great-great-grandfather Walters had. Drove sheep from Bathurst. B for Bathurst. Three weeks on the road. Three hours in the car, so far.

Eleanor started to laugh.

"Are you playing or not?" said Ken.

"Yes yes yes! Just hang on a sec. B. Ummm."

Blue, black, bloody, big, back...you're a big girl now. You know your father and I have always wanted to go back. B for bed. Sit on the edge. Don't whisper, Mum. Don't tell me this. Like periods. I don't want to know. Don't want to go.

"Eleanor, if you're not bloody-well playing, say so."

"I was playing, but I'm not now. Play by yourself. B's a stupid letter, anyway." She looked out the window.

"It is not," said Ken. "We're going to live at Barbarong and it starts with B."

"It's a stupid letter and a stupid place."

"Shut up the pair of you." Their father half-turned from the driving. "We're only a quarter of the way there and you're carrying on already. And you've woken Billy up."

Sit back. Stare out the window. Gum trees. Bloody gum trees.

Billy rubbed his fists in his eyes. "Watcha doing, El?" He pulled his sleepy body up beside her.

"Counting gum trees."

"How many you up to?"

"One million, forty-five thousand, nine hundred and eleventy-two."

"Mu-um, I'm hungry."

"We're stopping in Gunnedah."

"But I'm hungry now. I've been hungry since Armidale."

"Well you can stay hungry, Ken. It's only another half an hour. Play another game with Eleanor."

"She's reading."

Eleanor stared at the page.

Spotto. That's his next game, I'll bet. He always wins. Spotto cow, calf, caravan.

Eleanor and her mother crossed the road to go behind a tree.

"Are you all right, love? You're a bit quiet today."

"I'm OK. When are we going to get there, Mum?"

Her mother stood up and straightened her skirt. "About five. Watch out for the bull ants' nest." She paused. "You'll love it, El. There's a creek and a huge yard to play in and your own room and a verandah that goes right round."

"Do you reckon there'll be snakes?"

"Probably."

It was much hotter now. Her bare elbow rested on the window. New dark-chocolate freckles burned through the fine gold hairs.

"C'mon, El, play Spotto. Be a sport."

"Oh, all right."

She took the card.

Roadside mailbox. Easy. Woman on a bicycle. In this heat? What a joke. Cars, cows, trees. Number plate beginning with K.

"Spotto a cow and a calf. Down that gully. You missed it."

"Come off it, Bill," said Ken. "You can't have it unless someone else sees it too. That's the rules."

"But I did so see it. Hey, Mum, did you?"

"I saw it," said their father.

"Gee, thanks, Dad. That's beaut."

"And you can play more quietly. It's hard driving in this heat."

Their mother turned around. Sweat ran down the pale skin under her arms.

"Come on, we're all hot. Let me help. There's a car coming up behind us. What's its number plate start with? You look, Bill."

"It's N."

N. New kid. Bash up the new kid.

"Never mind. Maybe the next one. There's a tractor and a woolshed. You need them both. Mark them off."

"I bags the tractor. I was going to say it when you did."

"You can all have it. I saw it for all of you." She turned back to the front, kicked her thongs off and fanned her legs with her skirt.

"Spotto a level crossing," shouted Eleanor.

They bounced over the railway lines into a wide, flat town.

"What's that, Dad?" Billy pointed to three huge cement buildings.

"Wheat silos," his father replied. "It's all wheat out here."

They stopped next to a truck with kangaroo bars, parked outside the pub. Dad went in to get the drinks but Mum opened the door to catch the breeze and stayed in her seat. Eleanor, Ken and Bill got out and leant on the telegraph pole, close to the car.

"We should get a new one," said Ken, resting his foot on the bumper. "If we had a new Zephyr, we'd be there by now. Austins are rubbish."

Eleanor wasn't listening. She watched two girls sitting in the gutter in the shade of an empty cattle truck. A blue dog lay in the dust.

Billy tugged at her T-shirt. "Hey, El. See that building?" He pointed to the School of Arts. The paint peeled from the raised letters: "Est. 1870." "How old will I be when it's a hundred?"

"You work it out," said Eleanor. "Ten more years."

"Sixteen," he whistled. "Cripes, El. You'll be twenty-two." He paused for a minute. "Then you'll be left home and I won't have to sit in the middle."

They drove the long, straight road in silence. Eleanor's knees stuck to the green vinyl. She screwed her eyes to look back the way they had come. The mountains weren't there.

She closed her eyes.

Don't forget. Won't forget.

She swayed with the car, fell against Billy. He fell on Ken. Eleanor laughed.

"Get off." Ken pushed them both, hard.

"Quit it, Ken." Eleanor pushed him back.

"Well, you get over your own side." He drew an imaginary line between them.

"God, you can't take a joke any more."

"What is it this time?" Their mother turned round.

"She's on Bill's part and he's on mine. See. They're taking all the room."

"Tattle-tit."

"Move over, El. Stay in the corner." Her father caught her eye in the rear-vision mirror. "Jesus, I don't know why you kids can't sit still."

"They're tired, Jack."

"We're *all* tired."

Eleanor watched his reflection. Red dust eyes. Brown sweat forehead.

"...and if there's one more crack out of either of you, I'll stop the car and put the lot of you out. Your mother and I'll go on our own."

Good. Stop. Let us out. I'll go back. Walk back. Wee wee wee wee all the way home.

She was squashed between the sun and the road. There was no home now. The road narrowed through flat brown paddocks. No cool green mountains. No trail in and out the pine trees. No treehouse at Mick's place. She flopped into the corner as they turned at a signpost.

"Look, that's the river over there. We're following it. Doesn't it flow slowly under those big trees. Look, El."

"Is that on our place, Mum?" Billy leant over the front seat.

"Look, El."

"I can see it from here." She saw the sun, trapped in the lower branches of giant gum trees.

"This is the last turn here. We're off the tar. It's the farm road."

Eleanor bounced against the door. Her mother stretched her hand back and touched the girl's knee. "Here's the gate. Why don't you get it, love?"

"I don't want to."

"I'll get it." Ken slammed the door. He struggled with the heavy chain and then, one foot on the bottom bar, swung the gate wide open to let them through.

The house squatted low in the red afternoon light, earth-coloured water tanks on either side. Its dull cream walls were blistered. The car moved on, across the house paddock and stopped. Ken and Billy leapt out and raced to the front door.

"It's locked!"

"Have you got a key, Mum?"

"Jeez you're slow."

"Hurry up!"

Eleanor didn't move. Her father stretched back from the wheel and pulled off his wet shirt. He didn't say anything. Her mother sat, tapping her fingers for a moment on the dashboard. Then she swung the door open and he got out to follow her. He put an arm across her shoulders and they went towards the house.

Eleanor stood beside the car. Her big toe curled a pattern into the dust. She screwed her eyes up against the sun and turned to face the east. She looked past the pepper tree and the fence; the direction they'd come. The mountains were not even a line on the horizon.

"You coming in or are you going to stay in the sun all day?" her mother called from the verandah. Eleanor grabbed her thongs from the floor of the car and, without stopping to put them on, went into the house, banging the screen door behind her. Inside it was cool and dark.

"El!" shouted Billy. "Come here for a sec. The verandah goes right round and there's two sleepouts, one for us and one for you, and there's a block outside for killing chickens, I bet and the outhouse's up the back..."

She followed him into the kitchen and stopped. It was just like her mother had said. A big black stove set back with a side seat. She used to sit there and read when *she* was twelve.

"Tea, El?"

"Thanks, Mum."

Over the seat the shelf for warming things and a big black hook hanging down. It was all still there.

"Here you are. There's no milk. And take this one out to Ken. He's around the back somewhere." Her father handed her the cups and leant back against the sink, dust rings round his eyes. Her mother moved about the kitchen. She opened doors, looked in cupboards, touched things. She picked up a copper fruit bowl from the mantelpiece and rubbed it shiny against her hip.

Eleanor blinked in the glare as she stepped outside. She squatted on the top step with Ken and Billy and looked around.

"Bet that creek goes for miles and miles," said Ken, pointing to the winding trees below the fence. "Hope it's got enough water to swim in. D'you reckon it's got snakes and leeches?"

"Dunno." Eleanor sipped her tea.

Billy stood up and peered around the corner of the house. "How come there are no animals? You can't have a farm with no animals."

"Mum says they're all in the paddocks. One of the neighbours has been share-farming since old Harry went to hospital."

Trust Ken to know the details.

He threw a stone high up and over the pepper tree. "Hey, El, d'you wanna have a look at the creek? Come on, Bill."

Mum's voice came from the kitchen. "The wireless is working. You'll get the tail end of the Children's Hour."

Eleanor called out, "No." She shook her head at Ken. She put her hands deep into the pockets of her shorts and lay back against the warm cement of the step. Through half-closed eyes she watched the dust from the boys' feet disappear into the low rays of the sun.

Late that night she lay on her narrow bed. It was too hot for covers and she stretched her body beneath the sheet so that her toes hung over the mattress. There were moon-shadows on the wall. She sat up, listening. Cicadas; frogs; mopoke; no wireless. Everyone was in bed now. Boys around the far side. Hall down the middle. Mum and Dad at the front of the house, on the left. Dry, old smell. Pinewood burned in the other house. Read by the fire. Flannelette sheets.

I've had a bad dream, Mum. About the tin mine. Big black hole on the Red Range road. Water and snakes. Can I come in your bed? Just this once more. Snuggle down. Keep still. You'll wake your father.

Eleanor got out of bed. She tiptoed across the room. She crept along the hall to the front and peered around the open door. Two bodies, still beneath the white sheet, feet dangling.

I don't know why you can't sleep in your own bed. Christ, you're not a baby any more. You'll be at high school next year.

She pulled back, pressed herself against the wall.

Find me, Mum. Get up to go to the toilet. Check the boys are covered up. Please find me.

Don't worry. There'll be nice friends like Jane and Ruthie.

But Enid Jones says kids out West are bigger. Knew a kid once from Bathurst who could run faster than anyone in the whole State. That's nonsense. And I won't know where to go on the first day and which door is for the girls and which door is for the boys and where is out of bounds...

She waited. Cicadas and breathing and moonlight.

She shivered.

2

$\mathscr{M}$r Grant, the Headmaster, met them in the corridor. He wore shorts. The hairs on his legs were thick and black. Their mother followed him into the office and shut the door.

"He looks all right, Ken," said Billy. "Better than old Williams."

"Couldn't be worse." Ken pointed at the trophy cabinet. "Look at this shield. Four times in the last five years." Tennis, football, silver boys with cricket bats on varnished wood. Eleanor turned away.

She stopped under a painting, donated by the Mothers' Club, 1949, and stared at the white gum trees and the purple horizon.

"...d'you reckon they'll let us little blokes play?"

She caught her fingers in her belt and then smoothed down the navy pleats. Her hand felt in her pocket for her hankie, a small coin tied in the corner. Lunch money.

Who will I sit with? A gang? Like before? Bags us the big table in the weather-shed.

"...and they've won this one for the last five years. Bet they haven't got anyone can bowl as fast as you, Ken."

The door behind them opened.

"Have a good day," said their mother. "Don't worry about the bus. I'll pick you up." She smiled. "See you later." Her green skirt swung over her tanned legs as she went out into the sunshine. The double doors swung back into place behind her.

"Well boys!" The headmaster leant on the glass cabinet. "Your mother tells me you're keen on cricket. You'll like it here. Best cricketing school in the district, even if I do say so myself. We might only be a central school but we've beaten the full high schools in our time. See that shield there..."

Eleanor bent to pick up her case.

Keep talking cricket. Talk till the bell goes.

What if they've done Africa and Japan? And they still read Enid Blyton? What if no one collects autographs?

"Come along to cricket practice at lunch time." He spoke to Ken. "You're in the High School section. First year." He touched Billy lightly on the back of the head. "Come and watch. You're never too young to learn."

Her stomach hurt. Like waiting for a tetanus booster with the whole school watching. *Don't cry. Babies cry.* Like when the doctor took the splinter from her bottom when she'd bounced on the wooden seats at the baths.

" Sixth class. Miss Wily. A nice group. We'll go there first. You boys wait here. Have a look at the football trophies. We play a lot of football in the winter."

Goodbye Ken. Goodbye Bill. Good luck. I'm going first.

They were already looking in the cabinet. Their heads were bent together, backs to her.

She ran a little to catch up. Down the corridor. Turn right. Through a door and down some steps. Along a verandah. Two empty milk crates and a door marked "Library".

"That's the girls' playground. Someone will show you the toilets at recess. Cafeteria is over there. Infants' block is next to it. High School is on the top floor. Here we are."

There was a tiny glass window in the door.

"Seven eights are fifty-six.

Eight eights are sixty-four."

The ruler crashed down on the desk.

"Good morning, 6A."

Feet shuffle as bodies slide out of the seats. A pen falls on the floor.

"Good morning, Sir."

Girls in grey cotton pinafores stare at the new girl in blue.

"This is Eleanor. Eleanor Wheeler. I'm sure you are going to welcome her into the class, make her feel at home. Yvonne? No one sitting next to you? Right." He pushed Eleanor forward and gestured to the class to sit. Yvonne, in the front row, had long fair plaits that hung over her shoulders.

"Thank you Miss Wily. Good morning, 6A."

"Good morning, Sir."

The teacher turned her back to close the door.

"What'd he say her name was?"

"Where d'you come from?"

"Eleanor. Funny name."

"Where d'you live?"

"Quiet! All of you! The next girl I catch talking will move to the boys' side of the room." Miss Wily banged the ruler against the edge of the teacher's desk and smiled at Eleanor in the front row.

"It's the eight times table again. We always begin the morning with revision. Some arithmetic to sharpen the mind. Ready? I said *stop* talking."

"Once eight is eight.

Two eights are sixteen..."

Eleanor said the words automatically. Her eyes flicked sideways. Goldfish bowl, adverbial clauses chart, the familiar smell — chalk and varnish and hot kids. Black hair. Brown hair. Blonde. Not one other redhead. No freckled arms. She leant back into the rounded wooden panel that joined her desk to the one behind.

"...five eights are forty..."

The ruler swung down, up, down. Miss Wily's hair was cut short. She wore bright-orange lipstick which shone as she spat the words out. White roses, browned at the edges, huddled in a bowl on her desk. On each down beat she stepped sideways till she reached the wall chart near the verandah door.

WILDFLOWERS OF THE WESTERN REGION. THESE SPECIES ARE PROTECTED. THEY MUST NOT BE PICKED.

"...nine eights are seventy-two.
Ten eights are eighty..."

A girl under the window with short black hair smiled at Eleanor. Behind her in the corner was another girl who looked about thirteen. She grinned too. Eleanor started to smile back but the girl poked her tongue out, screwed up her eyes and nudged her neighbour.

"Watch me please, girls."

"...eleven eights are eighty-eight.
Twelve eights are ninety-six."

"That," said Miss Wily, stepping away from the wall and growing taller in the heat, "was an a-bom-in-a-tion! I can see that our new girl knows her mental arithmetic. My word, we're going to have to pull our socks up."

"Sssssss."

"Ah?" She put one hand behind her ear and arched her eyebrows. She strode down between the rows of desks. "Did I hear something?" She paused by the back row. "Get that stupid grin off your face, Danny Stewart." Whack! She brought the ruler down hard across his shoulders. He pulled away. She jabbed him with her forefinger. "That goes for all of you. Up straight. I don't care how hot it is. We are going to look like young ladies and gentlemen. Aren't we?" She slapped at someone's leg stuck out in the aisle. "Aren't we?"

"Yes."

"Yes, what?"

"Yes, Miss Wily."

"Thank you." She sat down at her desk and peered over the roses. "That will be enough for this morning. Take out your Social Studies projects and if I hear one unnecessary word..." She pointed at Danny Stewart. "Move into your groups."

Yvonne picked up her books and went to sit with the girl under the window. Two boys joined them. Everyone was moving. Miss Wily leant forward. "Just watch for today, dear. It's the last day on Japan. We start Africa next week. You can join in then." She went to a group at the far end of the room. Eleanor stared at the desk. DEL LOVES JIMMY. TRUE.

Always up the back, before. Eleanor, Enid, Jane, Ruthie. Creeps sit up the front. Dumbos to do the messages.

"Have you been to Sydney?"

Eleanor looked up at one of the boys from Yvonne's group. "Yes." She moved nearer to them. "My grandmother lives there. We went last Christmas. She lives at Bondi and we watched television. She's got three channels. Have you been?"

"Nah." He shook his head. "My Mum says it's too far. We go camping up the Warrumbungles instead."

Eleanor frowned. Warrumbungles? She'd never heard of them. He kept colouring the sea between the Japanese islands. "Helen's been to Sydney. She's gunna get TV soon. Her dad's building a giant aerial in the backyard and then we're all going over to watch it."

The girl with the short hair looked up. "He hasn't started yet," she said.

From the corner of her eye Eleanor noticed the older-looking girl in the next group. The girl mouthed at her, "You think you're smart. Danny's going to get you." She pointed at the boy. He winked and spat on his hands and rubbed them together.

The bell rang.

"When we come in we'll have reading from the magazine. Quietly!"

"Meet you up the back."

"Save us a seat. I'm going to the cafeteria."

"Get us an apple, will you."

They pushed and shoved their way past her.

"He's going to get you. When you're not looking." The girl dug an elbow into Eleanor's ribs and ran out onto the verandah.

"That's Kaylene," said Yvonne. "Watch out. Her brother's a policeman." She sucked the end of one plait. "That's the girls' toilet over there. You can't go past the bell. That's for the High School kids. You can go on the grass, but not with a ball. Milk's in front of the cafeteria."

"No," said Eleanor. "I hate it. We got green stuff at my last school. They said it was banana but we called it sick."

Yvonne screwed her face up. "That's my baby sister over there. My mother says I have to look after her." The plaits bounced as she ran off.

Eleanor hooked her arm around the verandah post and swung out over the asphalt. The wood scratched her.

Creep. Only creeps sit up front.

There was grass on the other side of the playground. Then a huge square of black tar to the bike sheds. More grass. Big kids played cricket. Ken, probably. Three girls from her class stood under the pepper trees. Helen, with the short black hair, was counting: "One potato, two potato, three potato, four. Five potato, six potato, seven potato, more."

She wanted to walk over, put her fists out, be in the game.

You count to a hundred while we all hide. Coming, ready or not. Eleanor, Enid, Jane and

Ruthie. The J. E. E. R. gang. Written on badges of red cardboard. Up the back. Run through their silly game. Crazy Enid. I'm the leader and you've got to do everything I do. Jump the swing. Run to the bike shed. Touch the bell post. Kick their marbles. Hold your breath and count to fifty. We're the gang and no one else can join. Jane, Eleanor, Enid, Ruthie.

Helen finished counting. She turned round. A smaller girl with her left arm in plaster began to trace on Helen's back.

"Draw a snake upon your back, who tipped your finger?"

Eleanor walked along the verandah, her hand bounced off the posts.

"Tinker, tailor, soldier, sailor, rich man, poor man..." She jumped as a ball struck her on the back of the knee.

"Mine!" A little girl screamed. She grabbed Eleanor round the waist to steady herself. "Sorry." She let go, picked up the ball and hurled it across the playground.

"Get out of our game."

"Watch out. You're on my square."

"Sorry. I'm sorry." Eleanor half-ran to the grassy spot. She turned her back on the playground noise. She sat in the shade of a gum tree and pulled her skirt down over her knees. Out in the street an old woman with a corgi on a lead came out of the corner shop. Eleanor leant back on her elbows and picked at the grass. A ladybird crawled along her black shoelace.

"Ouch!"

"Told you I'd get you." Danny Stewart's foot pressed her hand into the grass.

"Elea*nor* smell some *more*." Kaylene stood behind him, sucking a green popsicle. She laughed.

"Get off!" Eleanor shouted at him and tried to pull her hand free. "You're hurting."

"An' I'll hurt you some more. Smart-arse.

Come in here. Suck up to Wily. Think you're bloody great." He put his fingers in his belt and let his weight roll forward. "An' don't yell out for a teacher." He dropped on one knee and pushed her back onto the grass.

"Leave me alone!"

Don't cry. Don't cry in front of them.

"You should think yourself lucky they can all see. Or I might really do something." He pinched the soft flesh above her knee and yanked the skirt of her tunic. The pleats flattened. She swung at him with her free hand. He laughed and jumped up. Eleanor fell on her face on the grass. He slapped his thigh and ran off. Kaylene followed him behind the bike sheds.

Eleanor tried to move her fingers. They were red and sore. She rubbed them against her cheek and then stuffed them into her mouth and ran across to the bubblers. She put her hand over the top and turned the tap on hard, head bent forward as if to drink. Tears ran over the bruises and water splashed onto her tunic and legs.

The bastard! The bloody, bloody bastard.

A skipping rope slapped on the asphalt behind her.

"I saw a nanny goat, hanging out her petticoat. Swish. Bang. Fire."

3

"How's school?" Her father stood on the kitchen table. He swept the ceiling with broad swings of the mop.

"It's OK."

"What about these Western kids?"

Eleanor squeezed the rag hard. Dirty water ran over her fingers, cool, into the bucket between her legs. She shrugged and dipped her hands in, up to the elbows.

"And the work? Is it hard?"

She looked up but his back was to her.

"It's easy. Tables and stuff like that." She twisted the rag and shifted her weight onto the other knee.

Five days at that place. Five days of bloody Wily, Danny Stewart. 6A. Thirty hours, take away Friday afternoon sport.

She turned to the bricks around the fireplace. The big black hook hung there in the centre. She ripped a cobweb down and slapped water onto the bricks. Black rivers ran down her hands. They stopped, caught in the tiny pores, welled up and flowed again.

"Eleanor, get us some more water, will you? Christ it's hot up here." He mopped his face and wiped a hand across his bare chest. The mop dripped over his shorts. "You know," he said, as she picked up the bucket, "you're not giving much away."

"There's nothing to tell, Dad."

Outside the yard was empty. She filled the

bucket slowly, letting the water splash over her wrists and hands. Her skin dried as she stood up and flicked the drops of water into the dust.

"Can I do my room now?" Eleanor put the bucket on the table and took a step towards the door.

"Not yet. I want to get this finished. Sweep the cupboard under the sink."

She leant on the cupboard and traced her name in the dust. In running writing with curly loops at the ends.

With Jane in third class. Writing their names in the dirt on the Red Range Road, just before they put the tar down. The edge of town. Four hundred miles away.

"Dad, if you built an aerial in your backyard, could you get television from Sydney?"

"Dunno, it's a helluva long way. You'd be better off waiting till we get a channel on this side of the mountains. Why?"

"Kid in our class reckons her dad's building one." She looked up at him. "Anyway, how come we aren't living in town like before?" She reached forward into the sink cupboard. "Yuk, it stinks in here."

"Money doesn't grow on trees, you know," said her father.

"But isn't he coming back?" Her voice echoed in the tiny space.

"Who?"

"Uncle Harry."

"Not for a while. He's pretty sick."

"Is he going to die?"

Her father bent down and squeezed the head of the mop between both hands. "Get on with it, El. We don't want to be all day."

He returned to his scrubbing. She swept a dead mouse onto the newspaper on the floor. Its tail draped over the picture of Dawn Fraser, grinning at three world records.

"Are the kids here Argonauts?" Her father stretched his back and put the mop on the floor.

"I haven't asked them. I'm not listening any more. It's kids' stuff."

He looked at her, curiously. "Don't worry about the move too much, El. It'll be all right. We moved a lot when I was a kid. In the Depression. It was hard on my parents. Not like your mother's family, sitting pretty here."

Eleanor ran her finger along the funny U-shaped pipe in the cupboard and pushed the broom into the furthest corner.

"Six different primary schools. I had to fight for the first week every time. I remember one kid... holy terror, he was. He stopped... Hey, El, you haven't been in any fights, have you? You're not getting picked on?"

She backed out of the cupboard. "I need more water. I'll get it."

The afternoon sun hit her in the doorway. She hopped from one foot to the other on the burning step and splashed dirty water down to cool it. Sweat trickled from the creases in her elbows. Her T-shirt bit under her arms. It squeezed her chest.

"Watch this, El!" Ken flicked the hose and a jet of water went high in the air, then spattered down over him. "Look." He was in his swimmers. His body was suntanned, his brown hair streaked blonde. He threw the jet higher. Up. Up. "Come on. Come and get it."

But you've got to wear a shirt now. It's different. You're a big girl now.

Drops of water fell back to earth. Precious water.

The water hit her. Hard in the chest. Stung her eyes. Plastered her hair down.

"Quit it! Stop it, you bastard!"

Ken, the sun, the water. Ken laughing and

laughing. She hurled the bucket. He ducked, sprayed her hard in the back. She ran up the steps, into the house. She slammed the bedroom door and fell down, soaking on the bed, crying and holding the pillow to her.

Spoilt bastard, doesn't care. None of them care. They'll be sorry when I'm dead. Brave girl. Bitten by a tiger snake. Hit by a fallen tree, like Judy. Saved her little brother. They stand around the bed. Weep. Look at her pale face, closed eyes. So young. Ken cries. And Mum. And Dad.

She pressed her forehead into the mattress and dragged the pillow over her head.

Jane didn't have a brother. She had her own bookcase, all to herself. Straight black hair too, parted on the boys' side. She had a bunk in her room, just for when Eleanor came over to sleep.

Eleanor rolled onto her back and the wet sheet clung to her legs. She heard voices in the kitchen. Someone shouted and then the screen door banged.

"El?" Billy's face pressed against the window.

"Clear off!"

"Ken says it was only a joke. He says he's sorry and Dad's blown him up for wasting water."

"I don't care."

"Mum says we can stop now and go to the creek and have watermelon. Ken says you can have first go with the tire."

She turned her back on him. He gave up waiting and she heard his footsteps going back around the house.

Someone tapped on the door. "It's me, dear. The others are ready to go. I'll wait for you."

"Don't wait, Mum." Her eyes were red from crying.

"Aren't you coming?"

"In a sec."

"Are you all right?"

"Yes."

"You're sure?"

Footsteps went back along the hall. Eleanor stayed lying on the bed. The hot breeze had dried her skin and she moved on the wet sheet to cool her body again. There was a pool at the creek with a long rope to swing out on. You held onto a little wooden bar and jumped from the rock. It was just deep enough. Mum said sometimes it dried up enough to walk across. There'd be watermelon to suck, and grapes.

She swung her legs onto the floor. In the mirror, her wet hair stuck straight up. Orange freckles stood out from her white skin. She ran her hand down the front of her body, pressed the slight curves. She poked her tongue out and flicked water from her hair onto the glass. Her face and body were shattered, broken, running drops down the mirror. She couldn't bear to watch. She kicked her shorts into a corner and pulled on her bathing suit.

The wet sheet was heavy but she bunched it up and struggled with it onto the verandah. She flung it high up, over the line. The damp body shape flapped in the hot wind as she crossed the paddock.

She took the side track.

Better to swim to them. Casual. I've been in the water for ages.

She picked her way over the sharp stones and bindies, down to the creek's edge. There were gum trees and bushes and rustling in the long grass. Her thongs fitted neatly onto her hands and she slipped into the water. It was so cool. She heard splashing and calling further down. She pushed off from the shady bank, into the sunlight, duck-dived into the middle of the current, rolled onto her back and let the water carry her to them.

4

"*Wheee...*" Eleanor raced along the bare verandah boards. Her left hand dropped onto the rail and she flew up high and over it. She rolled into the dust and dead grass. The soft red powder clung to her shorts. Up, onto the verandah outside the boys' room. "I can fly!" Past the front door. Up, over again. She caught her toe on a dead rosebush, fell and cracked her funny bone. She laughed, then swore. Onto her back, laughing, nursing her elbow. The sun was laughing.

"Are you bloody crazy?" Her mother slammed the screen door. "Are you trying to break your neck or something?" She stood with one hand on her hip. The other waved at the empty yard. "We're stuck out here, your father's in town with the car. I've no truck, no telephone. You break something and what am I supposed to do? Sit out here, waiting like your grandmother when little Jimmy died?"

Eleanor sat up. "Who was Jimmy?" She brushed the pebbles from her leg. "What are you talking about, Mum?"

"Just get up and go and find something to do. I'm busy." She slammed the door again as she went into the house.

Eleanor followed her into the dining-room. The table was covered with china, photographs and the glass vases from the mantelpiece. The heavy brown curtains were dumped in a heap in the middle of the floor. A large cardboard box stood on the table and her mother was carefully wrapping each object in a sheet of newspaper from a stack on the table and packing it away.

"What are you doing, Mum?" Eleanor leant over and read the headline: "Margaret Engaged. Princess to Wed Commoner." She picked up a pencil and sketched a pair of glasses over the face below the headline.

"I'm having a blitz on old Harry's stuff. It can go back up when he comes home," said her mother. Eleanor began to colour in the pearls in the five-strand choker around the princess's neck. Her mother held a photograph to the light and rubbed the dust with her thumb. "Pity the water's got into that one." It had a silver frame and a flap at the back to make it stand.

"Is that you, Mum? On the horse?"

"No. Your Aunty Jenny was the rider." She pointed to the small figure peeping out from behind a man's trouser leg. "That's me. And that's Harry. He must have been about thirty then."

"And Jimmy?"

"Who?"

"Jimmy. The one you said. Is there a photo?"

Her mother leant back against the sideboard. "It's too long ago, El." Her left hand held a tiny china lady. The blue dress was cut low and the full skirt lifted to show layers of pink petticoats. She held the figure by one leg and picked up the sheet of paper.

"He was my brother." She half-wrapped the figure. The princess and her fiancé disappeared.

"Your *brother*!"

Her mother nodded. "I had two, not one. Jimmy was the eldest. In her old age your grandmother talked about him a lot. He could ride, swim, shoot. A real country kid and he had her red hair. He fell from his horse when she was pregnant with me. He died two days later." She touched the hair on the china lady. Tiny yellow roses held the ringlets back from the milk-white face.

"She sat by his bed and waited. It had been raining and the creeks were up and they couldn't get a doctor. No one could get through. Then they couldn't get an undertaker. She laid him out herself, wrapped in oilcloth. When the water went down, they took him in the back of the sulky. His body bounced round on the rough road. She cried all the way."

"Did he break his neck?"

Her mother finished wrapping the figure and stuffed it into the box. "I don't know. I was never told." She tossed a bunch of plastic grapes on top of the curtains and ran her fingers through her short brown hair. "I wanted to come back here, to the old house. Your father wanted to be in town, close to work. I like it here, in the bush. I'm damned, though, if I'll suffer the way she did." She waved her hand at the photograph over the fireplace. It was the only one she hadn't removed. "She was your pioneer. And her mother before her. You won't find them in your history books." She closed the box.

Huge brown eyes looked straight at the camera. Pearls, eight strands, rose from the smooth bodice. Her long hair was wound round her head. She was bride, princess, queen. Her tiny gloved hand rested on the shoulder of a man with a big moustache, beside her. She seemed not to notice he was there.

"You're a bit like her, El. The eyes, of course, and the colouring." She balanced the big box on her hip and moved towards the doorway. "I always said you weren't a Wheeler."

Eleanor started to go after her. The brown eyes followed her. She picked up a lace doily from where a vase had been on the sideboard and spread it over her short red hair. She tilted her head back, looked down her nose. Down the outstretched hand, fingers elegant, jewelled. Short, stubby, freckled, broken nails, bare scratched knees, torn shorts. She snatched the doily from her head, rolled it into a tight ball and tossed it onto the mantelpiece beside the photo.

In the kitchen, Eleanor poured herself a long glass of ginger beer. She dropped ice cubes into the drink and went into the front bedroom.

"How come the creeks were up, Mum? It never rains here." Her mother was standing on top of the bedroom stool, pushing the big box back on top of the wardrobe.

"Oh, it does rain sometimes. And when it does..." She gave the box a final nudge. "We always had enough food for weeks on end. When that ran out," she turned around and grinned, "there was mutton and damper." She climbed down and glanced at the mirror. "Let's see how tall you're getting." Eleanor stood beside her. Her head reached her mother's shoulder. "You're nearly up with me." The voice softened. "You are like her. I'm not." She pushed a strand of hair back from her forehead and patted her stomach. Her arms and legs were suntanned and her feet were bare. "Just a few bulges." She grinned at her daughter.

"Do you remember little Jimmy, Mum?"

"I wasn't even born, El."

"Was there a big one?"

"Big what?"

"Jimmy."

"Godfather! You're as bad as Billy with your questions. Yes, there was an Uncle James. Your grandmother's brother. But no, he wasn't called big Jimmy. He's dead. They're all dead, except Harry."

Eleanor wedged herself against the verandah post. The rail was narrow and she wobbled a bit. She closed her eyes.

Dead boy uncle. Small boy on a big horse. The big horse rears. Up. Up. The boy falls. There's a man with moustaches and a woman in white. She's got a big belly and long red hair wound round her head.

Ken remembered one Christmas with Grandma. She had given him a stone with trilobites and eaten his spinach for him.

"You can't remember," Ken had said. "You were too young. I was five and you weren't even four. You've just heard the stories and you think you can remember. Stories. Grandma had a fight with Uncle Reg. She left her share of the farm to her brother Harry and to Jenny and Mum."

In the afternoon her mother dug a patch of garden at the front. She wore the stockman's hat that hung on the peg near the back door.

"I bet that hat's been there since you were a kid," said Eleanor, from her seat on the step.

"Could be," said her mother. She put her boot on the spade and pressed down hard. She turned the earth, then crouched to pull the weeds and throw aside the little stones.

"Nothing'll grow here. It's all dead, Mum." Eleanor picked up a stone and threw it over the fence, into the long brown grass.

"You'd be surprised." Her mother leant on the spade. "All along that fence we had tea trees. There were bottlebrush and oleanders. Mum was a fine gardener. She could make anything grow."

Her mother pointed, past the dry brown grass and patches of rust-coloured earth. The bush began there, huge grey-green trees over saplings and scrubby bushes. "She wasn't just a gardener. She knew all of that. We used to go for walks with her and she'd teach us the names. Every tree and flower."

"But it's boring. It's all the same."

"Only when you don't know it. You'll find out. Get me the wheelbarrow and help me move this rubbish."

"I don't like gardening." Eleanor stood up and threw another stone. It hit the water tank with an empty ring. "I'm not like you two."

"Stop it! If you don't want to help then find something else to do."

Eleanor picked up a stick and started to run around the yard. She dragged it behind her, making crazy patterns. Giant figures of eight, an ant trail to nowhere. She drew an enormous wobbly snake and a huge, staring eye in the dust. The eye watched as she put the stick between her legs and galloped to the fence and back.

"Did she ride, Mum?" Eleanor flopped down on her knees.

Her mother nodded. "Why? Do you want to learn?" She wiped the sweat from her forehead.

"No."

Eleanor took another stone and hurled it into the orchard. It landed in the orange trees.

"Stop it, El. You'll ruin the fruit...and you should have a hat on."

"There's no fruit on them."

They sat on the step and her mother sipped a beer. Eleanor pointed past the twisted old trees.

"What are those buildings, Mum?"

"Shearing shed, that's the big one. Hasn't been used in donkey's ages. They used to sleep in the smaller one next to it. By the time I was growing up the shearers used to come out every day from town." She put the glass down and leant forward. "Oh El, you should have seen the dancing. The parties after the shearing. We had lights and a band. Over there." She pointed to the flat stretch between the shed and the orchard. "Everyone we knew would come." She turned to face Eleanor. "We'll do it again. It'll get better. We'll water the lawn with the washing-up and the bath. It might even rain and this old yard will be so green. We'll have an enormous party and you can invite all your new friends from school."

Eleanor bit her lip. She tugged at a piece of grass that struggled up through the cement path. It was tougher than it looked. Her fingers slipped off the yellow blade and her knuckle grazed a stone. A layer of white skin peeled back. She spat on it.

"I mean later," her mother said. "It's hard at first."

She pointed to another building which stood apart from the rest. "I bet you don't know what that one is."

Slab boards were nailed to a frame. It was squashed between the orange trees. Old, gnarled trees that held out their arms for a weird dance. Eleanor shook her head.

"The schoolhouse. Your grandmother and the other kids didn't go to school. It came here."

"Was it real? Desks and things?"

"They wrote on slates. The desks are still there." A tumbled-down verandah was tacked on one side.

"When I was about your age, I wanted it for a cubby. Mum wouldn't let me. We sneaked in there once, Reg and I." She grinned and hugged her knees. "We had a lovely time. There were books and clothes and all sorts of junk. We found some old readers. A is for Alcohol. D is for Drunkard. E is for Evil." She stood up. "Go and look for yourself. It's probably all there. I bet no one's ever touched it."

Eleanor stared at the buildings in the orchard.

Grandmother schoolgirl. Grandmother gardener. Mother of my mother.

Little Eleanor sits on the verandah. There's a ginger kitten. It hides under the house. Come on, Puss, Puss. Play with Elly... Sshh. Come on darling. She wants to see you. Gran wants you specially. Say goodbye. Sshh. She's not very well. Upsadaisy. On the big bed. Soft red cover. Huge brown eyes. Face lost in long white hair. Kiss. Bye bye to Grandma. Byeee...

Eleanor pushed herself off the step and went towards the schoolhouse.

5

*T*here was no handle. She pressed her shoulder against the door and pushed. It stuck. She stepped back and kicked aside a loose verandah board. Just a stick now, really.

Never pick up a piece of wood until you've kicked it over first. Watch out for redbacks.

The board fell over the broken step. Underneath it was black. Fat white spiders' eggs clung to it like round dew drops on the leaf of a rosebush. She took one end of the board and bashed it against the wall. The tiny eggs rained down around her feet. She threw her shoulder against the door. It broke open and she stumbled out of the brilliant sunshine.

She sniffed the darkness. One hand gripped her stick, the other stretched out and touched the dark shape in front of her. Leather. A saddle. Her palm ran over the smooth curve to the seat. Down the straps, over the buckles to the hard metal stirrups. She'd never been so close to one before.

She touched a small table under the saddle. Her fingers caught in a thin ridge at one end. A desk. School desk. Her eyes were getting used to the yellow-brown light. She stepped forward, slowly, felt two desks pushed together. It really was a schoolroom.

"Ugh!" She grabbed at her forehead. Fine, sticky cobwebs.

Never pick up a piece of wood until you've kicked it over first. Never put your hand down in the shed until you can see exactly where it's going.

Eleanor rubbed her forehead and then wiped her hand on her shorts. She tiptoed forward, testing the floor with the stick. Her sandshoes made no sound. "Bugger!" Her knee caught on the jagged edge of a tea chest. She touched it gently. No blood.

She scraped the floor with her stick. No slates, no readers. She lifted it and wedged the tip under the lid of a desk. She leant back slowly to pry it open. Slam! Back! Quick! Rat! Big as a rabbit. It leapt to the floor and darted between her feet, out into the sunlight.

Shaking, she stepped up onto the teacher's platform, back from the desks. Orange freckles stood out from her white knuckles. She lifted the stick high, held out her arms to the empty room.

"That," tap, tap, tap of the stick on the wall, "was terrible. Only the new girl was trying at all." She went up on her toes, inclined her head to the front desk. The new girl, red-faced, hunched her shoulders in the front row. "I can see we're going to have to keep on our toes."

Sss, go back to where you came from. Don't cry. Don't give them the satisfaction. We're gunna get you. You can't run out of the room, you can't. Don't you tell. Once again, everyone...

Both hands seized the stick. She swung around. Faster and faster. The stick crashed against the wall. Smash the blackboard. Bash the floor. Damn. The stick shattered. She dropped to the ground, her head down, arms round her knees. She rocked backwards and forwards, crying.

Someone was watching her. Eleanor opened her eyes. The desks were empty. She turned her head. There was no one at the window. The same smoky light filtered through the cobwebs. She flexed her back and swung her legs down, over the teacher's platform.

No snakes. No redbacks.

She reached out for the stick. It lay broken into little pieces on the floor. Without thinking she picked up a chip and crushed it between thumb and finger.

Something *was* there.

She looked hard into the four corners of the room, then stood up.

Don't be stupid. It's nothing.

Her sandshoes padded softly past the tea chest, the chairs, till she reached the sunlight in the open doorway. Suddenly, warm and brave, she spun round. She wasn't leaving. Her rust-coloured hair matched the pieces of old leather. Her hazel eyes ran over the rough slabs, each wall in turn. Cobwebs draped floor to ceiling. Then the beams. Three heavy, blackened logs. Across and back, across...

"Ugh!" A dark, furry shape in the corner.

A possum. Possums don't come out in the day. A bat. Bats aren't furry. Not like that.

It moved. Eleanor jumped. Eight long, furry legs. She held the doorpost, ready to run. Body as big as a bird. Spider.

Don't be scared. They don't bite people.

It hung, an upside-down umbrella, on the rafters.

She stepped from the doorway. Slowly, one eye on the spider, she skirted the desks, across the room to the window. She needed more light. She rubbed the glass with the back of her hand. The dirt smeared.

The spider didn't move. With a splinter of wood she hooked away the cobwebs and an old wasps' nest from the corner of the window. She spat on the glass and rubbed a hole big enough to see the house through. A dust cloud rolled along the fence from the road and then she heard the car. It slowed for the ramp, almost stopped, started again and came up to the house. Her father, Ken and Bill got out and slammed the doors.

Her mother dug the shovel into the ground and peeled off her gloves. Eleanor watched as her father went and spoke to her and then they beckoned Ken. He looked at the ground and shrugged. Her mother pointed at the schoolhouse.

Don't come and find me.

Ken shook his head and ran up the steps onto the verandah and into the kitchen.

"Eleanor?"

She slipped out of the room and shut the door. She ducked low under the branches of the orange trees, between the rails of the fence and approached the house from the shearing shed. Her hands were brown with a layer of dust, each hair coated with a fine powder.

"El-ea-nor!"

"I'm coming!"

Her father stood on the back step. "What happened to you? You look a sight."

Eleanor stopped at the water tank and rubbed her arms and hands as the lukewarm water ran over them.

"There's tea being made inside. Ken wants to ask you something."

She shook her hands dry and went into the kitchen.

Ken stood by the sink, pouring tea. He turned to look at her.

"Where've you been?"

"Nowhere."

He frowned. "We're going over to Mike Turner's place to fish for yabbies."

Eleanor turned her back on him and poured her own tea.

"He's a kid in our class. You can come too. His dad's going to bring us back round teatime."

They'd arranged it all. Eleanor hasn't got any friends. Take her with you, Ken. Babysit.

She picked up her mug and walked past him to the kitchen door. "No thanks."

The schoolhouse looked smaller than it had

34

when her mother pointed it out. The bark slabs were the same colour as the orange trees. It might have just grown there, out of the red soil.

"C'mon Eleanor," said Dad. "You're always moping around. Face as long as a week. Do you good."

"I don't want to go. You can't make me."

"Don't speak to me like that, young lady! No one's going to make you do anything. If you don't want to meet the local kids..." His voice trailed off. He sipped his tea thoughtfully for a minute. "Mum says you've been over in the old schoolhouse."

She didn't answer.

"What's that, Dad?" said Ken.

Their father pointed to the orchard. "That falling-down shack behind the orange trees. Your grandmother and her brothers and sister had school there. It's just a junk house now."

"Struth. In your own backyard! Get enough school all week."

Dad stood up and emptied the dregs of his tea onto the dirt.

"Ready, Ken. For the last time, Eleanor, are you sure you don't want to come?"

She didn't look round as they went back through the house.

She took rags from under the sink and a handkerchief of her father's from the cane ironing-basket in the laundry. She slid the broom under the handles of the buckets that she had filled from the tank. They were heavy and dragged her shoulders down. She stumbled on the rough orchard track and water slopped all over her legs.

Yabbying. Who wants to stand up to the ankles in greasy mud. Bitten by leeches. Ken showing off.

Eleanor kicked the door open. "Hullo spider," she said.

She tied the handkerchief over her mouth and nose. She knocked the saddle to the ground and kicked it over. No redbacks. She grabbed it by the hard front and dragged it onto the grass. Outside in the sun, the leather was cracked and dull. She sat on it. It was too big and she slid forward onto her back and then fell off. Back in the schoolroom she hooked the broom under a tangle of bridles and leather straps, held them in front of her and dropped them over the edge of the verandah. The sunny patch in the room was now empty.

She soaked the rags and sloshed the water over the window. Cobwebs and dust ran down the glass and into the cracks in the floor. The glass moved slightly at the pressure from her hand. Sunlight glinted off the rim of an old metal bath. It threw her shadow onto the tea chest. It lit up the dark corners and showed gardening tools, a rake, shovel and crowbar. She looked for the spider. It had disappeared. She stood quite still, shivered.

Stop being dramatic. It's out on the roof, eating birds.

She grabbed the metal rim of the bath and yanked. One end was higher than the other, like an old-fashioned couch. She dragged it across the room and over the verandah. It fell onto the grass. A little green bottle rolled clear of it, into the dust. She jumped down and picked it up. The sunlight bounced off a hard green ball in the centre. She spat on it and rubbed it against her shorts. The bottle fitted neatly into the palm of her hand. She held it up to the light and through the rich green colour she saw the outline of the doorway to the schoolhouse.

Not just a cubby. Push the desks to the walls. Cushions on the floor. Junk in the woolshed. Books. Real old stuff. Grandma's. Harry's. From the tea chest.

She put the bottle on the step and went to the door. The spider was climbing over the rim of the wooden chest.

Damn you, spider. Go back to the roof.

Her hands clenched. She looked for a stick. The spider lifted one hairy leg over the rich purple material that lay on the top of the tea chest. Eleanor picked up the broom and poked at it. She stepped closer as the spider touched a black lace-covered button and began to sink into the soft folds. She flicked at it with the broom handle. It waved two hairy legs at her. She poked again. It clung tightly, eight legs around the wooden pole.

She hurled the broom and the spider at the far wall. They landed on the teacher's platform. The spider ran up the corner post, into a space under the rafters. She tipped the tea chest over. The purple dress spilled onto the floor with suits and shoes, newspapers and books. She prodded them with her toe. Something else was packed firmly in the bottom. She kicked the chest. A parcel of yellowed material, someone's petticoat, landed on the pile. She knelt to unwrap it. Hard. A book. Red leather, old-fashioned handwriting.

To my Granddaughter,
    Elizabeth Emily Walters.
        On the occasion of her Thirteenth birthday.
        From her loving Grandmother,
            Charlotte Anne Walters.
            Manly.

                            20th September, 1895.

Her grandmother's diary.

6

27th September

My diary came in the mail this morning.
How did she know that I wanted one so
much? It is real, embossed leather. Father
said so when I unwrapped it on the
verandah this morning. 'For your secrets,'
he said, and winked across my head at
Mother. He thought I did not see him.
Well, I did. Furthermore, I shall hide this
diary from everyone. I shall take it with
me to the schoolroom tomorrow when
there is no one about. Perhaps I shall take
it with me to my secret place. That would
be a wonderful idea.

28th September

I am never, never, never going to marry.
There. I have written it in black and white
and nothing will induce me to change my
mind. It has been a horrid, horrid day.

'Up you get,' she said after lunch. 'Up on
the table. We are spending the entire
afternoon on the party dress and I want
none of your nonsense.' No one ever asks
me what *I* want to do. I climbed up on the
dining-room table with the lamp dangling
in my hair and the flies buzz-buzzing
around. The ruffle was tight and it
prickled my neck. It is all white and I look
foolish and insipid in white.

'Turn slowly around,' ordered Mother. I turned to face the window. Why, when you are on the table do you always want to scratch and fidget? Why, too, is it always such a glorious day outside? How dare Father agree with her and tell me that I was to stay at home with the babies. He went off to the far side of the run where *we* worked together yesterday. He was, in all probability, at that very moment swimming in the waterhole near the big rocks, while I was being tormented.

'You'll look a picture,' smiled Mother. 'We shall get some new ribbons for your hair and we can brush it a thousand times.' I do not want to look a picture; not like the one of the lady at the Government House Ball. Mother cut it out of the newspaper to pattern the dress. Ruffles at the neck, at the wrists and at the hem. It is so uncomfortably hot. I cannot imagine how unbearable it will be in November.

She is encouraging and she is a fine needlewoman and I suppose it is beautiful but I do not want to go and I told her so.

'You're an ungrateful girl,' she said. 'It will be lovely; not quite a ball, but a real dance. It will be like in Sydney or in Melbourne.'

I hate the idea and today I hate the Jamiesons for thinking of it. That is not really true. Kate is my second-best friend. We used to swim together and ride. Last year she came to help with the bottling but now they think they are high society. Sarah has put her hair up even though she is only fifteen. Tom is coming home for the holidays so the conversation is all dance, dance, dance. There will be cards with pencils tied with narrow ribbons and

I shall not know a mazurka from a polka. Even if someone asks me to dance, what shall I say?

'Besides,' said Mother, 'you'll have Edward to look after so you're sure to get some dances.' I suppose that is to infer that no one will dance with me but my cousin and I cannot abide him. He came last time when Uncle Tom went to Tasmania. He hardly even said one word, nor did he want to do anything I wanted. He has absolutely no love for the bush and so I have no desire to spend my time with him.

'Stop breathing!' she ordered. 'You're causing the hem to rise.'

'I can't stop breathing.' I am afraid I lost my temper and I stamped my foot and the table jumped and the pins fell all over the floor. 'I won't go to the dance,' I shouted.

'You will!' she cried. 'You will do just as you are told, young lady. You are uncontrollable and unwomanly. You run with the boys and the horses. You are *my* daughter, as well as your father's, and you will grow up to be a lady. I shall hear no more about it.' She put the pins in her mouth and the subject was closed.

But I am miserable. She understands nothing. Then the cows came in through the gate into the orchard. I saw them and leapt off the table. I gave her the Devil of a fright. She almost swallowed the pins. I cried out and hitched up my skirts and ran towards them. Mother ran too, waving her arms and her apron. The stupid beasts were running for the potato patch but we succeeded in turning them and securing the gate behind them.

Then we sat on the verandah and I laughed and laughed. It really was roaring fun. Mother threw her apron over her head and wept and wept. I was not sure what to do then, so I made her a cup of tea and served it to her in the good blue china teapot. I put the milk in the white jug which she uses only for guests and I carried it all out on a tray. We sat together like two old ladies. She mopped her eyes and said she was tired and who would be a woman out here in the bush. The dress had made her think of Melbourne and the life her sister has. She says I am growing up now and I have to help her more with the little ones and not go off on my own as much as I do.

In fact, I am to have another brother or sister. I know, although she has not told me yet. Last Sunday, at church, she and Mrs Jamieson spoke of it when they thought I was looking at the gold locket which Kate had received for her birthday.

I shall never be like her. I shall ride my horse and work the farm like a man and when the fancy takes me, I shall go off to my secret place in the bush. I am happy there.

I am writing this in the schoolroom. I came down here after tea. I am at Mr Saunders' desk because it is much bigger than mine. It is more comfortable too and it is lovely and quiet without Alice and Jake and Samuel.

What else can I write? There is a mopoke in the orchard. I suspect it is in the orange trees. School tomorrow. I have not completed the piece for Mr S. He will be displeased with me too. Why are not things like they were when I was Jane's

41

age? Why is everything so complicated now?

An elaborate, wavy line was drawn under the first entry. The fine, loopy handwriting blurred on the page.

Eleanor blew the dust off the diary. She put it on the floor in front of her and hugged her freckled, scabby knees.

Run to Mum. Look what I've found. Hide from Mum. It's my secret, my place. Secret place. What did she mean, secret place? Like the schoolhouse? Chasing cows. She did marry. She had Mum, Reg, Jenny. Little Jimmy.

She turned the page to the second entry. She hesitated for a moment, then closed the book and rubbed the soft leather cover. Embossed leather.

Slowly she wrapped the diary in its tissue and folded the petticoat around it. She placed it back in the tea chest and dropped the purple dress on top. She closed the door and then piled the saddle and bridles into the bath and began to drag it towards the woolshed.

After tea they lay on the floor of the lounge-room and played Monopoly. There was no breeze through the open door.

"Come on, Eleanor!" said Ken. "It's your go again."

She shook the eggcup. "One, two, three, four. Bond Street." Billy had two houses on it.

Which bedroom did Elizabeth sleep in? The sleepout? Was it built then?

"You were mad not coming, El." Billy rolled over onto his stomach and pulled off his pyjama top. "Look at my sunburn. I'm going to be real brown tomorrow. Mike reckons we can go any time we like."

"It's your go, Bill."

She looked through the doorway into the dining-room.

Stand on the table. Turn around. I look foolish and insipid in white.

"Yeah, El. Mike caught the most yabbies. He's real good at it. We had ginger beer and fruit cake before we came home."

Her mother sat in the big armchair, reading. The light picked out the red bits in her hair.

Soft yellow oil lamps. Did you go to bed when it got dark? No wireless. Read by a hurricane lantern.

"God, El. You're hopeless. Billy's landed on your place. You haven't even noticed. Play properly or don't play at all." Ken collected the fine for her and then threw himself out of jail. Eleanor tossed the dice, passed Go and collected £200.

"What did you do all afternoon, anyway?" Ken shook the cup.

Eleanor shrugged. "Nothing much. Found an old saddle. Just junk, I reckon."

"Hurry up, you lot. You've got school in the morning." Her father looked up from the book he was reading. "One more round and then that's it. Bed."

Eleanor finished cleaning her teeth and switched off the bathroom light.

Candles to light you to bed. Each person has one.

She closed her eyes and tiptoed towards her room. Her hands felt the knobbly wallpaper. "Ouch!" She cracked her toe on the edge of the bookcase.

"Eleanor, what *are* you doing? Aren't you in bed yet?"

She opened one eye a fraction, lined herself up with the bed and dived onto it.

7

"One, two, three, kick. Back, two, three. Walk away and back you come. Slide, slide, back, back and around you go. Ready. Boys, don't hold her as if she were a sack of potatoes. Girls, on 'walk away', let go of your partner, turn. Move on to the next one." Miss Wily beat time to the music. She took two steps and turned. The double strand of red beads bounced on her neck. "And girls, if you are a little bit taller, bend a little. Buckle at the knee."

Eleanor watched the crooked brown seam up the teacher's left leg.

Danny Stewart laughed. He had his hands in his pockets, five places ahead. He turned around and caught her eye.

She looked down at her shoes. Black, shiny shoes. Grey pinafore. Just like the other girls.

After Social Studies that morning Miss Wily had announced: "From now until the Fête and the school dance in three weeks' time, we will be having dance practice. I want no silliness or fooling around. Boys, before we begin, you are all to wash your hands."

Someone had poked Eleanor in the back. "Going to dance with me, Elly-Nelly?"

"Rack off, Danny Stewart, I hate you."

"Are we ready then?" Miss Wily clapped her hands. "Dancing is an activity we do because we are happy. We love to move to the music." The needle dropped onto the record and scraped.

"Everyone smiling now." She held her

hands out and stood high on her toes. "One, two, three, kick."

Eleanor glanced down at the little flecks of white on the shoulders of the boy next to her. He stood on tiptoe to reach across her shoulder to her hand. She didn't bend her knee. Her arms went up and down mechanically. She walked away, turned and came back to the next one. He was shorter too. Over his shoulder she watched the gardener, his back almost black from the sun, bend to fill the watering cans from the tank behind the girls' toilet.

"Back, back, and around..."

She closes her eyes and twirls. The long white dress flares. The ruffle lifts over her ankles. Her dance-card, held by a thin blue ribbon dangles from her wrist. He holds her at arm's distance. No dandruff. She spins. She cannot see his face.

"Ready."

She swung round to her new partner.

"What are you doing, Danny Stewart? You've moved." Her hands stayed by her sides. He had a little gold cross that hung in the V of his shirt. He looked straight at her.

"Come on." He put one hand on her waist and caught her wrist with the other. "Music's going to stop. I want to dance with you." She looked at the ground. The others all swung round once. He swung her round smoothly, twice.

"Don't move!" Miss Wily clapped again. "I want volunteers to demonstrate the waltz." She twisted her fingers in the beads. The gardener had finished watering. He leant back against the bell post, watching. Miss Wily took her handkerchief and wiped the sweat from her forehead. Her long orange fingernails pointed towards Eleanor and Danny. "How about you two?" She rested her hand on Danny's shoulder. "You were doing very well."

No! He'll trip me. He'll tread on my toes.

They'll laugh. I'll fall.

Miss Wily pushed them gently into the centre of the circle. "Have you got the hold right? Closer." The sun came off the asphalt and warmed Eleanor's legs. He put his arm around her and spread out his fingers, pressing them into the small of her back.

Dad teaching her to waltz on a Saturday night, in the hallway with the music on the wireless. The Albert Palais played "The Blue Danube". Just let me lead. Put your hand there. Relax. Watch out for the vase. Lovely.

"Now the count is one-two-three, one-two-three. Everybody watching? Wait for the music. Left foot first."

Danny Stewart pressed his leg against her pinafore and she moved back easily. One-two-three. Past Yvonne, staring. Past Kaylene, whispering to Helen. Eleanor forgot about falling. She felt the muscles of his back through his thin shirt. He grinned. Past Miss Wily, hands on hips. Teddy Johnston blew a long wolf-whistle.

"That's enough!" Miss Wily pushed them back into the circle. "That was lovely. Let's see everyone do as well."

"Not bad, eh?" Danny left his right hand resting on her hip. With his left hand he played with the gold cross. Eleanor stared straight ahead. Was this his way of saying sorry?

The music started again. He took her hands. "Lunchtime," he said, "I go up the back of the bike sheds."

Up the back of the bus kids hold hands. Boyfriends. She went with Mick to the treehouse once, on Saturday morning. They pulled a piece of bark off and the ants went crazy. He wrote her a love letter and she hid it in her drawer, inside a sock. He never kissed her.

The music stopped.

At twelve-thirty she emptied the books out of her case and put them under her desk. She kept her lunch and her library book and snapped the clips on her case down.

"Are you going with Danny Stewart now?" asked Helen.

"You're crazy," said Eleanor.

"Looked like it when you were dancing. You'd better watch out, he's Kaylene's."

"Kaylene can have him." They walked to the door together.

"He's out there now, waiting for her." Helen pointed to the bike sheds. Danny Stewart was leaning against the wall, hands in pockets.

"He kisses her behind the bike sheds."

He saw them, turned and walked deliberately around the back of the building.

"He killed a snake once. In the girls' weather-shed. A big black one. Kids were screaming their heads off. Wily just stood there and he got the shovel and chopped it up."

"I'm clearing out," said Eleanor. "I'm going to my father's office. Tell Wily, will you?"

"What's the matter? You can have lunch with us, if you like. Me and Kaylene, on the grass."

Kaylene. Kissed behind the bike sheds.

"Have you got George?"

"No. I'm just sick of this place."

Kaylene came from the cafeteria. She was sucking a red popsicle. Her lips and chin were smeared with it.

"I don't get George, yet," said Helen. "Kaylene does. Sometimes she goes home because it hurts."

"Just tell Wily for me."

Eleanor ran out through the side gate and turned down towards the river. She jumped over the cracks in the cement.

Tread on a crack.
Break your back.

Wagger. Wagger.

She'd never walked out on school before. She swung her case around like a windmill. There wasn't a cloud in the sky. She glanced back, quickly. No one was at the school gate and the street was empty. She ran to the corner of the paddock, threw her case over the fence and climbed after it. It rolled down the bank into a gully and she hitched up her pinafore to slide after it. Her knee banged against a stone. Blood trickled out.

George. It's not George, Mum said. And it's not any other silly name like the curse. It's a perfectly normal, bodily function. Like any other. It'll start soon enough.

But it hadn't, even though she went to the toilet every recess and lunchtime, just to check.

Eleanor walked slowly along the bank underneath the railway bridge. The tops of the summer grasses brushed her bare legs. She took off her shoes and socks and paddled in the creek. Tiny tadpoles darted out from below the round pebbles. Mud swirled up from the bottom as she tried to scoop at them. She gave up, stood perfectly still and watched a dragonfly that hovered just above the water. The sun sparkled through its transparent wings. For a second she caught sight of the rich blue body that shimmered and then darted across the water into the grass on the far side. She was left with her own reflection in the slow brown water.

She ate her Vegemite and lettuce sandwiches sitting crosslegged on a warm rock. *The Girl of the Limberlost* stayed unopened in her case. She stretched out in the sun.

Could you wag school when it was in your own yard? Did she go to the dance? What about Edward?

The hum of the crickets drifted over her.
What secret place? Where?
She closed her eyes.

Earthquake! Rumbling. Eleanor woke up, start-led. The Sydney train screamed overhead. She leapt up.

"Dammit!" She looked at her watch. Half-past three. The bus stayed at the convent till twenty to four. She pulled on her shoes and started to run. Up the bank. Through the long grass. Forget snakes. Over the fence. No one. She crossed the road and ran up the lane.

Miss the bus. Tell 'em I got kept in. Hitch-hike home.

Over the beer cans in the lane. Cross the highway to the red-brick convent. The fence was covered in rich purple bougainvillea. The bus was pulling out. She waved her hand. She ran and scrambled on just as old Dave leant forward to press the button that closed the door.

"Jeez, El." Billy moved over to make room for her. "Nearly had a heart failure. No one knew where the hell you were." Eleanor leant back and breathed deeply.

"Where were you?"

"None of your business. And don't you dare, dare tell Mum and Dad."

"Tell them what?"

"Just shut up! Cross your heart and spit." His finger moved and he spat on the floor.

"OK. I'll tell you after tea."

He looked out the window. The bus bumped and rattled over the potholes. She closed her eyes and held her case tightly on her knees. It bounced.

Little Jimmy. Bounced all the way to town. She cried all the way.

Eleanor lifted the diary out of the tea chest and put it on a desk. She unfurled the purple dress and shook it over the verandah rail. The dust tickled her throat and nostrils. She spread the dress on the floor in the doorway and settled back with the diary on her knees.

29th September

Alice was not the least bit sympathetic when I confided in her this morning. She was the first to arrive for school. She was on the swing in the orchard and when I told her about the dress she just swung higher and higher and tilted her head back until her hair brushed the grass. All she could say was, 'But it shall be a lovely party.' She is to wear pink with matching pink dancing shoes. I can see that she is already quite carried away with the idea of Edward's coming. She has obviously been speaking with Sarah and Kate. There is no one for me to talk to. I was relieved when Mr Saunders arrived and Jake and Samuel were not far behind. The lessons were their usual interesting selves (can I write *self* for a lesson?). I went to collect the eggs without a shawl today. Spring is properly here.

30th September

Mr Saunders and I had a fearful row. I raced Jake around the orchard, twice, with James and Alice and Samuel cheering us on. I beat him to tip the tree at the gate but my dress became wrapped tight around my knees and I stumbled for a moment and he overtook me. Old S. saw me from the schoolroom window and he used *very* strong language to upbraid me in front of the others. He indicated the tear in my skirt and my loose hair, and he reproached me for my lack of propriety. He said I did not know what it was to be ruled, and, as I am the eldest, I should set an example to the others. Who is *he* to speak to me like that? I held my tongue although the others were laughing, but inside I was boiling with anger. I could say nothing lest he tell Mother. I shall wear my riding trousers next week and challenge Jake again.

Eleanor glanced at her watch. Six o'clock. There was time for one more entry before tea. She put the diary down and stood up. She stretched her back. Everything was quiet. A flock of tiny birds came over the schoolhouse. They were black against the red sky.

"El!" Ken called from the woolshed. He stood on the roof, beckoning her. She shook her head and dropped back onto the purple carpet.

1st *October in my own place.*

Edward. Edward. Edward. That was all they could talk about at breakfast. There was a letter yesterday and he is to come early. I wanted to go to the paddocks again and Father looked at Mother and then said 'No'. He had egg yolk in his moustaches and Jane laughed. He said 'Sorry' to me when he left and then he suggested that when Mother could spare me, I go for a walk. Sometimes I think he knows about this place I come to — my own secret place.

'You'll be able to take Edward for walks

with you,' he told me. I shall not. I always come here and I shall never bring another soul. I would bring a sister, if I had one the same age. Jane doesn't count as she cannot even fasten her own boots yet. Sarah and Kate have each other. I complained of it to Mother once and she replied that I had a dear, sisterly friend in Alice. A friend is never the same. Alice would complain that the half-hour walk to come here was too arduous. I cannot imagine her scrambling up and over the ledge. A real sister would race over the stones with me and drink the water that runs over the rocks. I would explain to her that every time I get to the bend, on my way here, I imagine that the balancing rock has fallen and smashed the ledge. We could creep around the bend together and laugh to see it still there, as always, poised on its tip. I would pull her up onto the ledge beside me and she would explore the cave while I sat in the sun. If it rained we could hide deep in there until the clouds had passed and the rocks were dry enough to scramble down. I did that once and I had great difficulty explaining to Mother why I was not wet.

It is foolish to want what you do not have. The creek bed is full of wattle. I have a golden carpet here. The pink sky is my ceiling and the grey-green bush my walls. I suppose I should go back now. I shall walk along the bank and listen to the frogs. The sun is dropping down over the house. It is getting redder. It looks as if the whole sky and world is on fire.

Half an hour up the creek. A secret cave.
Eleanor closed the book and hugged it to

herself. It was too late to go looking now. She put the diary back in its place.

Her hands bounced off the knobby bark of the orange trees as she walked through the orchard.

A swing. Swing for Alice.

She reached the gate, climbed onto it and kicked the post. She swung out in a broad curve. A semicircle in the red dust. Bull ants scrambled down the walls of the deep ruts that followed the track from the orchard to the sheds. The sun glowed behind the house. Dust storms further out West.

The whole sky and world is on fire.

She jumped down and ran towards the house.

8

...Hand on her back. Swirl to the music. Slide, slide down the bank. Run. The long white dress wraps tight around her knees. She stumbles. They cheer him on. All of them along the railway bridge. They point. She falls...

Eleanor sat bolt upright. Sunlight fell on the sheets. Magpies called from the pepper tree. Dad in the kitchen slapped toast on plates and poured the tea.

"...It's seventeen and three-quarter minutes to eight. You're on the 2BR morning show and I'm your host, Jim Barnett. Stay with us for music, music, music..."

Dance music.

"Eleanor! Aren't you up yet?" Her mother stood in the doorway. "You'll miss the bus. Come on. The others are nearly ready."

"I feel sick."

Her mother crossed the room and opened the wardrobe. She took out a clean white blouse and held it out in front of her.

"What do you mean, sick?"

"I've got a pain."

"Where?"

Eleanor pulled up her pyjama top and rubbed her stomach. "Around here."

"And how long have you had this?"

"Since I woke up."

"Come on. Up you get. You'll feel better when you've had something to eat. I'll make you some toast."

"Oh, Mum." Eleanor fell back onto the pillow. "I will be sick when that bus hits a pothole. I'll throw up at school and I won't be able to get home." She rubbed her stomach again. "I'll have to stay in the sickroom."

"Hey, Mum." Billy ran along the hall and stopped at the door. "I can't find my PE shorts and Ken won't wait. What's up with her?"

"She's not well." His mother hung the blouse on the doorknob. "Where did you take them off?"

"Sick my foot!"

"That's enough. Come with me and look." She turned back to the bed. "Maybe you'd better not eat anything. I'll bring you some tea when they've gone."

Eleanor heard the screen door slam and the boys' feet run on the gravel. In five minutes the bus would bounce over Riley's bridge and stop at the gate. She pulled the sheet up to her neck. The door slammed again. She knelt on the bed to look out of the window. Her mother struggled down the steps with a heavy bucket. She bent over, scooped out a jugful and began throwing the washing-up water on the yard.

"The tea's weak and there's no milk in it so it won't upset your tummy. You've got a bit more colour in your cheeks." She closed the window. "It's going to be a scorcher again today. Ninety-eight degrees, the forecast said. The fire danger's high. I'll just go round the house and shut everything up. Yell out if you want anything."

Eleanor lay still. Looked around the room. The walls were bare. Her school case lay open on the floor.

Yvonne had a picture of Elvis Presley taped inside her case. Eleanor couldn't think of anyone to put in hers.

The room felt small, hot. She swirled her tea

in the bottom of the cup and drank it quickly. She got out of bed and found her mother in the laundry.

"Do I have to stay in bed? I'm boiling." The cement floor cooled her feet. Her mother felt her forehead.

"You haven't got a temperature. I suppose you could get dressed and come out here." She plunged her arms deep into the blue rinsing water.

"I thought I might go down to the school-house," said Eleanor.

Her mother didn't look at her. She slapped a towel down on top of the other wet clothes and plunged her arms in again. "Eleanor..." She hesitated. "One might be forgiven for thinking that you just didn't want to go to school today. One minute you're sick, the next you want to be running down to that shack. I thought you were starting to like school." She wiped her hands down her hips and turned round. "I hear there's a school dance coming up. Ken says practice has already started. He seems to be enjoying it."

One, two, three, kick.

Are you going with Danny Stewart now?

"I'm not Ken, Mum."

"I didn't mean that. Look. Your father and I try not to interfere. But if there's something wrong. If there's something you want to tell me..."

"There's nothing wrong. I've got a pain, here. It's hot. I want to go to the schoolhouse and read in the shade. That's all."

"Suit yourself."

Eleanor went back to her room. She kicked her pyjamas under the bed and pulled on her shorts and sandshoes. She slipped out the side door and walked across the yard. When she looked back the washing was in the basket on the path. Her mother was lifting the huge forked pole to bring the line down to her shoulder. Eleanor climbed the fence, ran through the orchard and pushed open the schoolhouse door. The spider was nowhere to be seen.

4th October

At last the dress is finished. Mother and I sat with it on the table between us and we each stitched on ruffles. It is a closed subject. I am to go but I will not enjoy myself and no one can force me to, against my will. At the dance I shall leave Edward to the mercies of Alice and Kate. I shall escape to the grassy ridge above the waterhole where we used to swim. I almost broke my ankle there once, running from Tom Jamieson. I suppose I shall be expected to dance with him, too.

8th October

Alice and I are somewhat estranged, ever since I told her my true feelings about the dance. I imagine she wishes she did her lessons at the Jamiesons' and not here. She can make the first step towards reconciliation; I certainly shall not. Alice is not my only trouble. In all of this past week I have been out only once with Father to work. I used to go so frequently. There has been a real conspiracy to keep me in the house. When we did go, the main topic of conversation was Edward and how I am to behave when he arrives.

10th October

Mrs Jamieson came to afternoon tea today. Sarah and Kate did not come with her. In fact, they have not been here for such a long time. Not that it perturbs me. 'Why don't you take the young ones for a stroll?' asked Mother. 'You always love to go along the creek on your own. Take them with you.' One moment I have to stay at home, the next I am being urged to go out. We did go towards my secret place, up to the right from the house and I confess I had a very real longing to take them there. I know, however, that once we were there, there would be a constant cry of, 'Lizzie, I want a horsey-ride' or 'Lizzie, I want to get down'. The silence that is so important to me there would be broken.

Instead, we walked as far as the first bend and then Freddie became tired and I carried him home on my back. Jane and James clung to my skirts all the way to the house. James did leave me at one point to catch a butterfly but he ran so wildly and he made such a noise that the thing escaped.

Eleanor skimmed each page:

... I argued again with Mr Saunders...raced Jake through the orchard and this time I was victorious...Sunday and church and as usual I am the nursemaid while they gossip...

Eleanor searched for particular words. "The dance"; "the dress"; "Edward".

30th October

Edward has arrived. He came on the mail cart this morning while we were at lessons. Mr Saunders had to let us out to meet him.

You would think that we had never had a visitor before, such a fuss his coming has caused. Mother clucked around like an old hen and Alice served him his tea. She is not even a member of the family. Everyone asked stupid questions about the trip. Then James tried to drag him off to see the newborn lambs. I must confess he took it rather well, but he fell asleep in the afternoon and did not wake up in time for tea.

31st October

Freedom at last. Mr Saunders has left! He announced his imminent departure at today's lessons. He is to go to Sydney to join his brother who is a merchant. It is too late in the year to engage another teacher, so the families have all agreed to an extra month's holiday. Of course, we all had to promise that we should attend to our lessons in that time, but the weather has been glorious and I can see that there will be opportunities to walk and ride and swim. Even Alice was happy. Mr Saunders relaxed a little and talked of his plans. He says he has to leave the bush. He finds it 'boring, oppressive and dull'. He is so typically ignorant of something which he does not understand. If he could only see it in all its splendid colour, from my secret place. But, of course, I shall never, never take him or anyone else there. No one shall ever see it.

The secret place. Secret place.

Eleanor's stomach rumbled. She glanced at her watch. Twelve-thirty. She put the diary back in its place and went up to the house.

"Well. Your appetite's recovered," said her mother. "How do you feel?" She fanned herself with a folded sheet of newspaper.

"A bit queasy."

"Go and have a lie-down. It's this heat. No one should have to work in this weather. We're crazy not having siestas like the southern Europeans." She waved Eleanor away from the table. "We can wash up some other time."

Her room was cool. Cave-like.

Half an hour up to the right from the house. Over stones. Round a bend. Climb to a ledge. Under a balancing rock.

"Are you asleep? I'm going to lie down a bit, myself." Her mother's bare feet padded along the hall.

Eleanor watched the flies buzz slowly round the light bulb. They stopped on the smooth white shade. She got up and put on her sandshoes. She waited for a moment in the open doorway. Her mother's room was at the front. The house was quiet. She stepped forward on the sides of her feet, silent, across the hall to the dining-room, the kitchen. The linoleum squeaked. She held her breath and eased the screen door open. The spring stretched without a sound. The wall of light hit her. She screwed her eyes up against the sun. Down the back steps and onto the drive. The heat burned her bare arms, bare legs, her neck. Sweat started to run down inside her T-shirt.

Elizabeth in a long dress, boots.

She looked down at her freckled knees. At the far end of the drive she unhooked the gate and leapt onto the bottom bar to swing through.

I would bring a sister. A real sister.

She jumped down to close the gate.

"Eleanor! Eleanor, where are you going?"
Her mother, hand up to shield her eyes, ran from

the verandah across the yard.

"I'm just going for a walk."

For a stroll. Up the creek. To the right.

"In this heat. It's over a hundred inside. You're crazy. You're supposed to be sick!" She swung the gate open and grabbed Eleanor by the arm. "You could get bitten, fall, collapse from heat-stroke and I wouldn't know where to start looking. You haven't even got a hat on." She hooked the chain over the gate. "Just you get back up to the house. I'm not joking." They stopped in the shade of the tank-stand. "You could die out there."

Die in a cave. No one knows. Sunstroke. Stroke of luck. No one shall ever see it.

"It is not the local park you're living in. It's dangerous if you're alone. You know nothing about the bush." She opened the back door. "Sometimes I think nothing has changed. Not a damn thing."

Who would be a woman in the bush?

"You're staying inside for the rest of the afternoon, where I can keep an eye on you. Put the wireless on. You used to love listening to the serials. What about Uncle Mac and the Argonauts?"

"It's childish. I want to read the book I left in the schoolhouse."

"All right. But hurry up and bring it up here."

4th *November*

Shall Mother and I ever stop quarrelling, and over clothes which are so unimportant? I feel that trousers are perfectly sensible garments to wear whilst riding and normally she does not mind. She was the one who made them for me last year. But because Edward is here she says I have to wear skirts. 'Oh, Lizzie,' she said. 'You are not to wear those. We agreed that while Edward is here you are to be discreet and womanly.' She cried again and I said that I had not agreed to any such thing.

'There's no harm in it,' said Father, for he was in a hurry to be off to the paddocks. So I wore my trousers and now Mother and I have fallen out even more.

I did not really mind Edward being there, although when Father and I are alone we have such jolly times. This morning Father must have felt obliged to explain everything. 'It's mainly for sheep,' he said, 'from here down to where the creek divides the paddocks.'

I rode in front of them and I stopped listening. The birds took my attention. There are so many galahs, and magpies too, calling all day long. Father left us at the Petersons' boundary. He had to go to see them about some cattle, and I rode home with Edward.

I did not know what to have a conversation about, with him. In the evenings he has been so quiet when we are all sitting around after the meal. Sometimes I have seen Mother looking at him as if she wanted to draw him into the family but is not sure how to accomplish it. But outside, today, he was quite different. A pink cloud of galahs screeched over our heads and he insisted we stop. 'Shall we sit for a moment and watch them?' he said. Then he began to extol the virtues of our home. 'You are so lucky,' he said, and he extended his hands in a theatrical gesture. 'There are no dark and sombre buildings, no bustling traffic and crowds of people going about their business without heed for their fellows. The seaside near Sydney is pleasant enough, but look at these trees. It is so peaceful. You are so fortunate.'

I have never heard anyone speak like that. I wanted to cry out in agreement, but I thought it foolish to reply. Instead, I took him down to the creek and taught him how to skip stones. He was not a very good pupil.

"Sam Turner's coming out to do the firebreak, Saturday." Eleanor looked up as her father put down his knife and fork and rested his elbows on the table. He went on, "He came up to me in the street this morning. Reckons he always did it for Harry but he's had a crook back and he's been laid up. Should have been done weeks ago."

"Hey, Dad. Can Mike come with him? I always go to his place."

"Ask your mother."

Ken looked across at her and she nodded. He spoke to Billy.

"Then we can see if there are yabbies in that dam. I just bet there are."

"Tell him to bring his pyjamas," said his mother. "He can stay and go in with you on Monday. It'll be nice to have him here." She looked at Eleanor.

"I don't care if he comes or not." She scooped her peas onto her fork. "Who wants to go yabbying, anyway?"

Ken rested his chin on one hand and watched his sister.

"Coupla kids asked where you were today.

That Helen and one of the boys, Danny Someone-or-other."

"What did you tell them?" She stuffed the peas into her mouth. Two of them fell off the fork and rolled under the edge of her plate.

"Said you were sick."

9

The tractor started up. Huge metal cutters dropped down to plough the soil. Forward and back. They ripped out the tussocks of dry grass. Clouds of red dust swallowed the machine, the fence and the yard. Eleanor watched from a tree in the shade of the orchard as a hot wind carried the dust over the house.

Billy ran from the verandah steps across the yard. He leapt in the air and waved to the driver. The dust blew into his hair and eyes and he ducked behind the thick trunk of the pepper tree.

She heard the back door slam. Ken and another kid came down the steps with the washing-basket. Mike Turner, as tall as Ken but with sandy hair and skinny legs. Eleanor stretched out along the branch to watch them. Ken dropped the pole to bring the line down. They unpegged the flapping sheets and charged at each other to fold them. Ken stood on his hands. "Hey, Mike, watch this." Mike walked on his hands, took four steps, then fell. They laughed, wrestling each other on the hard ground.

The huge machine cut between Eleanor and the fence. Giant wheels. Roaring engine. She hooked her legs over the branch and let go with her hands.

Trees. Fence. Red-dust sky.
No house. No Mum and Dad.

Her hands brushed the long dry grass. Her forehead and eyes felt heavy. The ground came up to her hair.

A swing for Alice.

The tree shook with the vibrations of the tractor.

"Gidday." Sam Turner, upside down, took one hand off the wheel and waved. Sweat ran over his bare belly. He laughed at her. She tried to wave back, but the branch wobbled and she grabbed at it to save herself from falling. The dust lifted away from the house. Her mother and father sat drinking tea on the front step.

Eleanor rubbed the grit from her eyes and went into the schoolhouse. She shut the dust out.

7th November

'Tell me about the Jamieson dance,' said Edward when we were fishing this morning. 'I enjoy dancing. It sounds as if it might be amusing.'

'No, it will not be,' I retorted. 'It will be full of people who think that showing off their best clothes is the highest form of human achievement! And they will have all their conceited city friends with them!'

He smiled, and I realised what I had said. He is not like that at all. I felt too embarrassed to look at him. Fortunately, James came up at that point and his line was all tangled. I bent my head and concentrated on unravelling it.

It seems we cannot quarrel for long. He changed the subject and we lay on the rocks in the sun and talked of school. I felt that the classroom and Jake and Samuel and Alice were a long way away. Edward says his father wants him to go to London in two years, when his schooling is finished, but he is determined to resist the idea. Fortunately, his mother has never wanted him to go. He is worried about his father.

Apparently he is quite ill and that is the reason Edward is with us. I think I would go to London. How exciting it must be to travel around the world. I cannot believe that the sun which warmed us on the rocks is now shining in some far corner of the globe. I told Edward as much and he threw his head back and laughed. His hair fell in his eyes and when he lifted up his hand to brush it back I realised how brown he has become since his stay with us.

I shall miss him when he has gone. We caught four fish. We banished Mother from the kitchen and we cooked them for dinner.

8th November

The trouble started when I said we wanted to go on a picnic today. 'What do you and Edward do when you go off alone?' asked Mother. She was bathing Freddie and I was leaning back against the chimney, holding the towel.

'Oh, nothing in particular,' I replied, rather airily. 'Usually we talk about school. He has told me such a lot about Sydney and I am teaching him all the trees and plants that you have taught me.'

'You know, dear, you are growing up. You are almost a young woman. Some people might think it wrong for you to spend so much time alone with Edward. He may be your cousin but he is still a young man.'

I suppose by 'some people' she meant Mrs Jamieson. I just looked at her in disbelief. 'But may we go for our picnic?' I asked.

'No,' she said, quite firmly. 'Your father

and I have talked about it and we think it is best if you don't.' She hesitated for a moment, then said, 'Of course, you could take Alice.' She looked pleased at this solution.

'Alice!' I cried. 'I don't like her. I can't abide her.' I dropped the towel and ran into the bedroom. Alice has never been a true friend for me. I have never been able to talk to her as I can to Edward. She thinks that the bush is a place to fear. For her, it is full of danger. She could never have watched with me, as Edward did two days ago, when the snake came. We were at the creek, on the bank, when the shadows in the boulders opposite us moved slightly. A snake, its head held so alertly, slid out of a crack in the rocks and then up and over the nearest boulder. We sat, frozen. I kept expecting to see arms and legs emerge to help it climb. Its long, thin body seemed to expand and contract, and with each movement of the muscles it gained a little more distance. It passed through a patch of sunlight and then disappeared into the shadows. We did not speak to each other about it.

I lay curled up on my bed like a child and I cried, but only a little. I was determined that I would speak to no one for the whole day.

I was silent, too, at dinner. The others chatted on about various things. Edward had spent the entire afternoon with Father.

'Why didn't you join us?' he said. Everyone was looking at me. I wanted to run out of the room, but that would have served no purpose. The atmosphere continued after the meal. I very determinedly put myself into the littl♦ chair near the door and turned away from all of them. I could hear Edward pulling out the cribbage board for a game with Father. Why, when everything was beginning to go so nicely, does something have to happen to destroy it?

"Eleanor." Mike stood on the step. "Hey, this isn't bad for a cubby. What are you reading?"

"Nothing." Eleanor snapped the diary shut, pushed it under the dress and jumped up. "Just an old book."

Don't come in here. No one. Not Ken. Not Bill. Not you.

"Is it an old shearers' hut?" He leant against the door frame, one hand in his pocket, the other picking at the splinters of wood. He didn't try to enter.

"Something like that." She walked past him onto the verandah. She put her hand up to shade her eyes. "Where's Ken?"

"We're going for a walk with your mum, up the creek."

Up the creek. Right from the house.

Ken stood on a fence post and waved a stick. "Hurry up!"

Eleanor and Mike crossed the firebreak. Their feet slipped on the newly turned clods of earth. Dirt spilled into their shoes. Her mother handed Eleanor a hat and she pulled it down hard.

She watched Ken and Mike from under the brim. They walked ahead, kicking the layers of long brown gum leaves and dried twigs. They made their own path between the trees, stepping around the short spiky bushes that grew waist high. Ken held aside the saplings with his stick.

"I'm a snake killer!" He swung the piece of branch hard against a solid trunk.

"Whack!

"Stop it!" his mother called. "Watch where you are going in the first place. Move quietly. You'll frighten everything away." Ken dropped the stick and walked behind them.

They heard the creek before they saw it. Cool sounds of water on stone.

"Boy! It's down." Billy looked at the water running over the pebbles. "You could walk across now." He looked at his mother.

"It's pretty low," she nodded.

Ken waved toward the left. "I want to go this way."

No. No. Right from the house.

"No," said his mother. "It's too open that way. You'll cook in the hot sun. If we go up the creek the bed drops and it's shaded." She led them along the bank. "It's ages since I've been here. I used to come with my mother. She taught us all the trees."

I am teaching him all the trees and plants that you have taught me.

Eleanor hung back and watched her mother. She strode forward, confidently. The loose edge of her slacks flapped against her ankles.

She must know about the cave.

Billy had run on ahead and swiped at a low branch. "What's this one then, Mum?"

"River gum," said Mike.

"Bull," said Ken and pushed him into the water. "It's a gum. It's in a river. So? What's its name, stupid?" He ripped a piece of the rough bark from the tree. Ants and beetles swarmed along the trunk.

"That's enough, Ken," said his mother. "He's right. That's its name. Do you know any others, Mike?"

The creek dipped. Eleanor followed the

others down the steep bank onto the boulders and pebbles beside the water. She was wet under her arms and sweat trickled down the backs of her knees.

"How long have we been walking, Mum?" She flapped the bottom of her T-shirt to cool her stomach.

"About twenty minutes."

Twenty minutes. Half an hour from the house. But alone. In a dress. Where's the bend?

"I'm hot, Mum," said Billy. "When are we going back?"

Freddie became tired and I carried him home on my back.

He scratched his peeling nose and stopped. "I wanna go now."

"Quit whining, you little squirt." Ken flicked him on the back of the head.

"Get out!" Billy swiped at Ken. "You're always picking on me. Just because you're bigger. I'm going back."

"Come on, both of you," said their mother. "No one's going anywhere on their own. There's a big bend up ahead. We'll stop there and you can all have a drink. Then we'll go back."

A bend.

Every time I get to the bend, I imagine it has fallen...the balancing rock...smashed on the ledge.

"Race you to the bend," cried Eleanor. She leapt across to a boulder in the shallow water. She jumped back in front of the two boys and ran along the edge of the creek. She forgot she was hot. They raced with her and caught her as the straight bank turned into a bend at a huge rock pool. They stopped. Mike reached into the water and splashed his face and body. "It's great!" He threw a handful over Eleanor who laughed.

"Where are you going?" he asked.

"Just around the corner. To see what's there."

He pulled off his shoes and socks and dangled his feet in the water. Then he lay back on the warm stones.

Around the bend. The creek bed straightened, then dropped again so that the steep walls moved in on her. Hot stones burned through her sandshoes.

If it had fallen. Smashed on the ledge. Sixty-five years. Any time. Any storm. Never find the cave, see the colour. The splendid...

A screeching pink cloud. Galahs, disturbed from their drinking. They flew up the creek bed, high into the trees, wheeled round and down onto a rock. A huge rock. Poised. Balanced on its tip. Glaring sun. Eyes shut. Stumble forward. She wanted to laugh. Climb to the ledge. Find the cave.

"Coo-ee!"

Dammit!

She spun around. Mike's voice. No one had come into sight. She put her hands to her mouth and answered the call. "Coo-ee!" She searched the bank for a path through the trees. Up again to her rock. It was hard and dark against the still blue sky. She hesitated and then ran back the way she had come.

9th November

We did go for our picnic after all. I awoke to find Mother drawing back the curtains and she kissed me, which is something she has not done for a very long time. Then she said that she and Father had reconsidered the events of the previous day. We were to check the sheep in the south paddock and count the lambs and then we were free. I could scarcely believe my ears.

It was a glorious morning. There was a

shimmering heat haze on the horizon. The animals were all too sleepy to look up at us and the sun was so hot that it urged us on to the water. The lambs were frisking about. For some reason the heat never seems to slow them. I told Edward how the hawks come and pick the eyes out and we agreed that it is a monstrous example of nature's way.

We ate so much. We had thick mutton sandwiches and fruit cake and lemonade. Edward pointed out that I did not want to see the lambs suffer but I was quite happy to eat them! I suppose he was right but I laughed and said that I thought it was not the same. We splashed each other with our feet which were dangling in the water. Then we had to lie in the sun to dry. The sky was such a deep blue and the clouds were just brushstrokes of white. I quite forgot Mother and Father.

On our way home we went near the secret place. I realised that I had not been there for a very long time. I stopped at the point where the track forks. It would have been so easy to take him there. I know he would have understood its wild beauty, the colour and the marvellous silence. He called out from behind me, 'Why have you stopped? Where are you taking me?'

'Nowhere!' I cried and I kicked old Whisky into a gallop. I wanted to fly and I charged across the paddock as if my life depended on it. I went over two fences and my hat blew down onto my back. My hair streamed behind me. The trees and the ground raced by at a cracking pace. I have never ridden so fast. I crossed the next paddock and the next.

I waited for him where the wheat begins. He came up, puffing and very red-faced. 'Why did you do that?' he demanded.

'I felt like it,' I replied, somewhat flippantly.

'Well, you scared me to death. Never, ever do it again.'

'How dare you tell me what to do!' I cried. 'You are not my master.'

He looked surprised and puzzled.

I turned Whisky towards the house and this time we did not mend our quarrel. How quickly it changes. One minute I have a mind to take him to the most secret, precious place and the next it is as if I cared nothing for him. It is all so horrid.

And the dance is only a week away!

*E*leanor lay in bed listening to the cicadas. She closed her eyes and planned the next day.

Beneath the balancing rock, rucksack on her back. She climbs to the ledge, turns, looks out over the bush. She takes the diary out. Opens it on her knees...

"Are you still awake?" whispered her mother. She pushed the door open.

Soft, confiding voice. Time we had a little talk, love...

"What do you want, Mum?" Eleanor propped herself up on one elbow. Her mother sat down on the end of the bed.

"Tomorrow the boys are going fishing. Billy too. El, I want you to go with them."

With *them*, tomorrow!

"Mum, I hate fishing! You know that." She paused for a minute. "I'll get sunburnt."

"Now, you listen to me. You were quite happy to get burnt the other day. They might be skylarking around. They've got no time for Billy. I want you to keep an eye on him. Be responsible."

Eleanor sat up. "But Ken looks after Bill. He always has."

Her mother moved to the door. "Look, El, you hang around the yard, day in and day out. It'll do you good to have a day out in the bush. You're *all* going after breakfast, and that's final!"

Tomorrow!

Eleanor clenched her fists. She punched the pillow hard and then picked it up and threw it onto the floor. "Damn fishing. Damn the bush. Damn damn damn!"

Shall Mother and I ever stop quarrelling?

Her body sagged. She flopped back onto the cool sheet.

"You're coming, aren't you?" Mike looked across the table at Eleanor. She nodded.

"We're going yabbying in the dam, and swimming, so you have to bring your bathing suit," said Ken. He rested his elbows on the smooth wood of the table top and stirred the glass of Milo.

"Why can't we go to the creek?" she asked.

"Dam's better."

Mike spread honey on his toast. His hair fell in his eyes and he flicked his head back. She lifted her feet onto the rung under the table and they brushed against his. He didn't seem to notice.

"We made meat and tomato sandwiches," he said, "before you got up. There's fruit and dates and cake."

Eleanor got up from the table. "I'll go and get my stuff ready," she said.

"Keep an eye on him, El." Her mother pointed to Billy. He sat on one side of the truck, his feet resting on a bale of hay. "Remember what I told you. Look out for snakes and don't leave any rubbish lying around. I've emptied the drinks into plastic bottles. Glass is too much of a fire hazard in this weather. You've got your watches so you won't be late. If you leave by about five o'clock you should be back in plenty of time." She handed Eleanor the lunch-bags. "I'm going to put my feet up for a while. You'll enjoy yourself."

Eleanor hesitated. The car horn tooted. She ran out of the kitchen and down the back steps.

The truck picked up speed. She stood on the

back of it next to Bill. They waved to their mother as she grew smaller and smaller. The ground whizzed past beneath them. The hot wind blew in Eleanor's face. Her hair streamed behind her, and she closed her eyes.

Soft, squelching mud oozed through her toes. She held the line with the bait in her left hand and threw it into the water.

"You've got to scoop with the net when it bites." Ken flicked his net to show her. "It's got to be real quick."

"I know. I know."

Catching tadpoles in the gutter on the Red Range road. Dad's hankie tied between two sticks.

She bit her lip and concentrated on the brown water.

"Got 'im!" cried Mike. Flick. Out. Into the bucket.

A tug on her line. She jerked her wrist. Missed. The water splashed up and over her shirt. She almost slipped. She dug her feet in harder. Mud swirled up to her knees. Another nibble. She scooped wildly. The yabby flew out onto the bank and thrashed around in the mud. She laughed and fell on her knees.

"Look what you've done!" shouted Ken. "It's too muddy. You'll scare them all away."

"Good!" she screamed at him and hurled the net away from her. "I'm hot. I want to swim." She dived out into the middle of the dam. First Billy and then the others followed. They rolled on their backs and duck-dived to the colder water below the surface. She opened her eyes. Murky brown silence. She could see nothing. A hand grabbed her foot.

Ken.

She kicked hard and swam to the warm surface. Mike bobbed up behind her. He disappeared again and then came up closer to the edge. Black mud clung to the hairs on his legs as he stood ankle-deep in water. "I'm hungry," he said. "Who wants to eat?"

There was a single shady tree a stone's throw away from the water. He trampled the grass down to clear a space and began to take out the sandwiches. Billy took the ice-cold drinking flasks from the canvas bags. He threw one to Ken.

"Aren't you coming?" Mike called to Eleanor.

"In a sec." She rolled onto her back in the water and drew her knees up to her chin. She flicked her cupped hands and somersaulted backwards. The water pressed hard on her eyes and forehead. She rolled sideways and thrust her legs down. Her face popped into the sunshine like a cork. No one was watching.

"Cold lamb or tomato?"

"Lamb." Her wet fingers made the bread soggy. She ate hungrily. Flies landed on her shoulders, forehead and mouth. She spun around to shake them off. The grass was spiky and scratched her bare feet. Ants swarmed over the crumbs which had landed on her dry toes.

"I reckon we should go down to the creek." Mike tipped his head back and sucked on the ice in the flask. "It can't be that far away and it'll be cooler." He threw the container to Eleanor. "I'm roasting out here."

"What about that place Mum took us to yesterday, Ken?" Eleanor touched her burning cheeks with the icy flask.

"That's miles away," said Ken.

"There must be other rock pools," said Mike. "We could find one, easy."

Ken shrugged. "Mum says there are some but it's a fair hike and they're all a bit dry. It's further to walk home in the end."

"Let's go," said Billy. "I'll walk real fast and keep up."

Mike went to the edge of the water to pack the fishing gear. "Can someone give us a hand?" he called.

Eleanor bit into her apple. "You go, Bill," she said. "I'll bury the scraps." She picked up a large stone and tried to dig a hole. The ground was hard. "Easier to burn them," she said.

"Not on your life," said Ken. "There's a complete fire-ban. Anyway, we haven't got any matches."

They followed the fence, single file: Ken, Mike, Billy, then Eleanor. She felt hot already. She scratched her sweaty scalp.

"Hey, El." Ken turned and walked backwards to call to her. "Mike says he had your Miss Wily last year."

"She spits when she sings," said Mike. He turned too and walked awkwardly in the narrow tractor groove. "Does she sing like this with you?" He raised his eyebrows, almost to the hairline. "Do, re, mi, fa," his lips pushed forward, "sol!" He spat the sound out.

Spit lands on the new girl in the front row. You have a charming voice dear. You must try out for the choir.

"La-a-a-ah!" He held the note for as long as he could. He waved his hand at Eleanor and Billy.

"Ti, do!" His face was red. "Come on, everyone." He conducted energetically. "God save our gracious..."

A silent black form glided across the track, behind Ken and Mike.

"Snake!" cried Billy. He stopped still, pointed ahead.

Mike spun around. He seized a stick from the side of the track, clutched it in his right hand. The snake's head disappeared into the long grass near the fence. Sunlight gleamed on the shiny black body.

"Keep still," whispered Mike.

Billy grabbed Eleanor's arm. "It's OK," she said. Her knuckles were white.

Let it go. Hurry, snake.

Mike jumped forward. The stick crashed down. Whack!

"Get 'im, Mike!" Ken screamed. Billy let go of Eleanor and clapped his hands.

The tail flicked up.

"Look at him. He's a beauty." Mike held the snake out to her, on the end of the stick. The body fell slack, torn by the beating. Eleanor stepped back. "Don't be scared," he said. "It's dead." He flung it over the fence. Head down. The pink and white of its underbelly caught on the barbed wire. She wanted to reach out and touch the scaly skin. A shadow passed over her, across the grass. A huge bird circled above them.

"I wasn't scared. It wasn't hurting you." She turned away. She wanted to get to the creek, quickly. The backs of her legs burned. The ground was too open. The shadow passed over her again. "Come on, Bill," she said.

Shady river gums spread down to the water. Eleanor and the boys dropped what they were carrying, kicked off their shoes and ran into the creek. Knee-deep. The red dust washed off their bodies. She swam hard to the opposite bank and then came back lazily. Billy stood, water up to his hips, staring at some object in the water. Ken swung his arms wildly. Sharp, stinging drops flew from his palms. Mike fought back.

"Eleanor?" called Mike.

She turned. Water slapped her cheeks, stung her eyes. He was laughing. She waded towards him, eyes closed, hands slashing. A wall of drops between them.

"El! El, I nearly caught a fish." Billy jumped, slipped and fell back underwater. He bobbed up. "I did, really," he spluttered.

Eleanor climbed out onto the rocks. Ken and Mike flopped down on their stomachs beside her.

"You coming out?" she called to Billy.

"No fear. I'm going to catch one for sure."

"You'll get sunstroke."

Billy ignored her. He concentrated on the tiny bubbles that rose to the surface.

"It's great here," said Ken. "Much better than our old place, eh, El?"

She scratched the rock with her fingernail. A lizard the size of her finger darted out of a crack.

"What about the trail?" she said. "You used to think that was great."

Slapping their thighs. Eleanor and Ken. Down the Red Range road. Over the Bishops' fence. We hate you Piggy Bishop. We're going to get you. Hurl the gravel at his new toy truck. Run. Hide in the gully. Under the bridge.

"It was a game we had." Ken stretched like a cat and spoke to Mike. "Years ago. We had this tree stump on a vacant block. Up the top was the crow's-nest and you could see right into the centre of town. El jumped off once and knocked her tooth out."

Mike skipped a stone across the creek. His hair fell into his eyes. He brushed it back with his brown hand. The hairs on the back of his wrist were white.

Eleanor threw a pebble to land near Billy.

"If you're not coming out, put a hat on. No one's going to carry you home if you're sick."

He stood up. His hair was plastered down over his ears. His nose was red. She threw a hat to him.

"Anyway," said Ken. "Some bastard cleared it. The block I mean. When we got back, last year. They'd put a bloody house on it."

"Couldn't happen here," said Mike.

"Nope." Ken got up to set the lines. Mike helped him tie on pieces of meat.

Eleanor watched them, her eyes half-closed. They were crouched together, weighting the ends. Talking.

"...reckon we'll get any..."

"...and my dad says..."

Talk to someone... I can talk to Edward... A friend. Not like Jane. Not baby secrets. But the feeling...on your own. Like Elizabeth. Edward.

"No. Mmm." Someone grabbed her shoulder. "Let me sleep."

"Eleanor. Eleanor, wake up. Please." Ken's face close to hers. "You've got to come!"

She sat up. Splashing sounds. Mike and Billy swam slowly towards the other bank. Ken grabbed her hand.

"What's up? What is it?"

He dragged her up the bank. The rocks scratched her knees. He hauled her over the edge and pointed. A column of smoke drifted up towards the sun. It began in the trees, far away to the east.

"Christ, El! What are we going to do?" he shouted. "It's a fire...a bloody great bush fire."

11

They slid back down the bank.

"Get out! Get out! We have to go!"

She pulled on her clothes.

Mike blew a jet of water through his teeth. He floated on his back and lifted one arm in a lazy stroke.

"Mike!" she screamed. "There's a bush fire."

He charged out of the water and onto the rocks. Billy leapt out and began to pull on his shorts.

"Where? How far?" Mike shook the water from his hair and grabbed one of the food bags. He bent to tie his shoelace. "Leave the lines." Eleanor had already taken the other bag and begun to drag Billy with her up the bank.

"Wow! Look at that smoke!" Billy gaped at the cloud. It filled the sky to the east. Over the cleared paddocks, the wheat stubble and the bush. From the blackening horizon it surged and lifted to a lighter grey. "Let's go back to the dam, El. Mum and Dad'll come there."

"It's the wrong way," said Ken. "They wouldn't make it in time." He looked around nervously. "They won't have seen it yet." He held his hand up to the wind.

"You don't have to test it," said Mike.

The morning stillness had gone. A hot wind blew against their faces.

"We've got to get home," cried Ken. "It's quickest 'cross country."

"No! We'll get lost," Mike shouted at him. "The creek leads home. Stay with the creek."

Eleanor watched the cloud. It was so far away. Surely that meant no danger. Suddenly, a mass of birds flew out of it. White cockatoos. They reeled and screeched along the creek bed. One hesitated in its flight, turned and came down to settle on the tallest of the gums. Then it changed its mind, flew up high into the blue sky and rejoined the group. The whole flock wheeled to the left, beating their wings. Faster and faster. The sunlight caught their golden crests. They swooped low over the scrub, across the next paddock and the next.

"Wish I had wings," said Billy. He rubbed his fists into his eyes.

Eleanor grabbed Billy's hand and started to walk. "We don't have to run. We can walk home along the creek." She shortened her stride to stay with him. He shook her hand free.

"Don't hang on to me, El. I can walk by my own self. When it comes, we'll go down the creek. We'll be all right under the water. It won't get us there."

Get into the water. Thin trickle. Fire all around.

Boil the kettle for afternoon tea. Hard boil.

She looked down at him. "It's not coming. We'll get home."

They crossed the half-cleared paddock. The creek was on their left. Eleanor's feet slipped on the uneven ground. Long grass brushed against her bare legs.

Snakes. Snake hole. Rabbit hole.

She pointed to the dust-brown sheep pressed up to the fence. Mike shook his head. They didn't speak. Save energy for walking. They hurried. Up, over logs. Around stumps. Home.

They'll come for us. They'll find us. The

wind'll change. It'll rain. Mum'll come in a Land-rover. An airplane.

She glanced up. There were no clouds. Just haze. High up, light grey and billowing, surging towards the sun. She sniffed. Smoke. She looked back. It was coming closer. There were no flames. It charged across the paddock.

She started to run. The hot wind rushed against her legs. Smoke prickled her eyes. They all ran.

"They'll be out looking," said Mike. His voice came in bursts. "Christ, they'll be worried stiff." He ran strongly beside her. She watched his arms pumping evenly. He kept glancing sideways at Billy.

Mum on the verandah. Hurl the bucket of water. Fight the fire with washing-up water.

"Hell!" Mike cracked his shin against a fallen branch. Tiny beads of blood. "Trying to be smart." He laughed, limped for a few strides and then ran again. They were out of the paddock and into the scrub. They crashed through bushes and saplings. Little bushes crumpled under her sandshoes and then sprang back. Tough, knee-high branches slapped her shorts, tore at her skin.

"It's too slow like this. We should cross the creek. It's clearer there." Her voice stuck in her dry throat.

"No fear!" said Mike. "It's too open. It's burning much faster there. Don't worry. The flames are always way behind the smoke."

How do you know? How do you know?

Billy ran hard to keep up. His smaller body ducked beneath the branches which she swerved to avoid. His mouth was shut tight and his eyes fixed straight ahead. She kicked at the undergrowth. Twigs, branches, leaves. Waiting to burn and burn and burn.

Eleanor's legs hurt. Her chest hurt. Sweat ran down the side of her nose. It trickled into the corner of her mouth. Salt. She tried to breathe slowly, deeply. Her eyes smarted. She rubbed them with the back of her hand. Tiny black specks covered her skin, trapped in the pale hairs. Ken's shirt was black. There were black streaks in Billy's white eyebrows.

"I've got a stitch," Billy said. "It hurts." He held his side.

"Come on," she said. "You can rest in a minute. After that gully." She pointed to a fence where the ground dropped sharply away. Dry grass and bushes grew thickly over the side. Ken held the wire. Bill went first. Eleanor tossed the food bag ahead of her. The barbed wire grabbed at her T-shirt, scratched her back. She ducked to free it. So much time for a fence. Mike stayed to hold the wire for Ken.

"Watch how you go," he called. "Don't break anything."

They slid and fell, tumbling over dead logs. Eleanor grabbed a bush. She bounced against a shrub with spiky thorns. There was a sharp pain in her shoulder. Caught. She wrenched free. The sleeve of her T-shirt ripped away. She lost her balance and rolled through the burrs, the sticks, over the stones to the bottom. Head down. On all fours. She pushed herself into a sitting position. Her shoulder was sticky with blood.

"You went too fast." Billy slid against her. "I got scared halfway so I stopped." He stood up and rubbed the seat of his shorts. "I came on me backside." His back pocket hung by a couple of stitches.

"We can't get up there." Ken pulled the cat's eyes out of his palm and waved at the other side. "It's too steep. Waste of time. Let's go in the creek bed. Follow that." They hesitated.

Eleanor grabbed Billy's hand again. "Come on, along the creek." He didn't pull away. He tried to keep up. His face was red, his lips apart and gasping for air. She had her breath back. They ran along the edge of the water. The tall banks sheltered them from the hot wind, the smoke.

Tomorrow. Tomorrow it will be a bad dream. Nine o'clock tables. Ten o'clock Social Studies. Eleven o'clock dancing.

She kicked a stone in her way. Everything was running. Rabbits, rats, mice. On each side of the water, the grass rustled and surged. The banks were moving, hissing, squealing. She breathed heavily, smelt burning leaves and wood. Burning hair, fur.

The whole earth moved around her.

A searing wind roared along the creek bed. It whipped her hair. Ash stung the creases in her knees, the tear in her shoulder. It pushed her forward. She stumbled. Billy fell with her. He grabbed at her, his eyes wide open. Both hands clutched at her arm. He cried out as they fell hard onto a flat rock.

Eleanor struggled forward and dropped her arms and face into the water. She gulped down great mouthfuls then turned, pushing herself up onto her elbows. Beside her, Billy crawled forward, arms outstretched, clumsy. She saw him tremble, then his body doubled up and as she lunged forward to grab him he tumbled into the creek. His head struck the bottom. His arms jerked and the small body slid forward.

"Ken!" screamed Eleanor.

Billy floated, face down in the water. She leant out, seized him round the waist and tugged at the weight. Her arms ached. She jumped into the water and lifted his head. "Get up! Get up!" She slapped his face and, putting her body under his, heaved him onto the bank.

"Let go. You're hurting," he whimpered. His head dropped forward. Water ran from his hair and eyes, over his nose and chin. It left black ash streaks. "I'm stopping here." He closed his eyes.

"Like hell you are!" Ken bent down and lifted him onto his back. Tears ran over Billy cheeks.

"We'll take turns," said Mike. He took Ken's arm and guided him over a fallen trunk. He cuffed Billy lightly on the back of the head. "We'll make it, mate."

Eleanor's feet squelched in her wet shoes. The smoke came down the tunnel of the creek. Billowing, choking smoke. Blinding smoke. Eyes, hair, nostrils. The sun disappeared. In the darkness there were logs to trip over. Huge, low, menacing branches.

"My turn," said Eleanor. She pulled Billy's arm across her shoulder. He was too heavy to carry. She held him tightly, bent low. Her legs jarred with every stone.

A big tree cracked behind them. Dead wood hurtled over the bank, down into the cutting. Flames shot through the bushes and licked the grass. There was fire in the rocks. Fire like flickering Christmas lights.

"It'll get us!" screamed Billy. He slapped Eleanor's back and tore her hair. "We're going to burn and burn." He pulled away from her. His weight dragged her down.

I carried him all the way home.

"We'll have to hide," Ken looked round, frantically.

Mike took Bill's hand. "Come on, mate, my turn."

A place to hide. Safe. Secret place.

The darkness closed around them. Huge, wild darkness.

"Ken! Mike! There *is* a place!" She grabbed Ken's shoulders, screamed into his face. "How far are we from the house? The place we went with Mum, yesterday?"

He looked at her blankly, tired. "Not far, I think. We've been running for ages."

"There's a cave. It goes right back. Under a balancing rock, on this side."

They didn't move.

"I'll find it!" she yelled. "I'll take you there. Bring him!" She let go of Billy and darted ahead. She splashed through the shallow water and onto the rocks. Run, run. She glanced back. Mike and Ken supported Billy. One arm each. He dragged his feet. One shoe was gone. They strained under his weight together, their red faces barely visible in the dark. There were flames behind them. Fifty yards, forty. Her eyes streamed. Smoke. Tears. It was in her mouth, her lungs, her stomach. She wanted to throw herself down. Sink under the earth.

Behind her, they stopped. Billy fell to the ground.

"You're crazy!" cried Ken. "There's no cave." Tears streaked his face. "Mum would've told us. You're mad. You've never been here."

"There is! There is!"

"He can't make it." Mike knelt beside Billy. "We have to stop. Get in the water. Get all wet. We have to." Words gulped through tears.

"We'll die! Die!" She shook all over. Hands clenched. "It *is* there. I know it. She told me. You'll boil. The smoke. The steam. You *know* that, Mike Turner."

Flames, thirty yards.

Sparks landed at her feet. A tuft of dry grass caught alight. She stamped on it. "Come *with* me. I *know*." She could hardly see them for smoke.

She ran, watching the top of the bank. The huge trees swayed, groaned against the wind.

Don't miss it. Lost in smoke. Help us. Help, Grandma.

There was a pain in her chest, noises like thunder in her ears.

Please.

She saw rocks, trees, boulders, smoke, rocks. A huge rock. Taller than the trees.

The balancing rock.

"That's it!" she screamed. "It's here." She

stumbled towards it. The boys came out of the smoke. Eleanor spoke in short, sharp bursts.

"We have to climb." Her throat cracked. "Push Billy after me. Then Ken. You last, Mike."

She plunged into the scrub, gripped the trunk of a small sapling and pulled herself up. Her fingers burned. Her feet skidded on the dirt and little stones. Pebbles rolled back onto Billy. She held on with one hand. "Come on! We're nearly there." She took his small hand. It clasped hers weakly. She yanked him up by his wrist and wrapped his arm around a tree. "Billy! You've got to try!" In the semi-darkness she saw a soft purple swelling under his left eye.

Look after Billy. You're responsible.

Hot tears ran down her cheeks.

She wedged her foot into a space. She pulled his arm, his shirt. "Push him, Ken. Push!" The hot wind came again. Roaring, screaming wind. It tried to pick her off, lift her, drop her in the creek. She clung to the ledge above her. One hand gripped the collar of Bill's shirt.

Grandma. Grandma.

She scrambled forward. Her hands were raw. They slipped on the sharp edges.

You said there was a cave. There must be a cave.

Up. Over. She grabbed Bill's hand. His face came up to the rock. Blood trickled into his hair. She reached down, under his armpits. She tugged. Her knees slipped. "Help me, Billy. Use your feet." She arched back. Heaved. They fell together into the mouth of the cave.

12

"*No!*" screamed Billy. He stared at the black mouth. "We'll die in there."

"We'll die here if we don't!" She gripped one arm and dragged him forward, on his knees. He tried to free himself from her. He punched her in the chest and ducked beneath her arms. She seized his shirt. Smoke blocked out the creek, the trees and the sun.

Ken's face came over the edge of the rock. "Get in there, Bill. She knows what she's doing." He shoved his little brother from behind.

Eleanor crawled forward, slowly, one hand holding onto Billy. The cut on her shoulder split open. She blinked in the half-light and strained her eyes to see. Black. Nothing.

Is there a hole, a drop? Bottomless pit?

She spread her fingers and felt for each step. Grains of dirt stuck to her palms. Sharp stone edges caught under her fingernails. Jagged pieces of rock tore at her knees. The smoke teased the back of her throat, burned her eyes, her nose. Billy sobbed behind her.

"It's coming in. I can't breathe." Mike choked and pushed forward. Ken and Bill fell against her legs. Her shoulder hit the warm powdery wall.

A tightness squeezed her chest. She tried short, sharp breaths and suddenly felt dizzy. She groped in the blackness. Her shoulder bashed against stone. Pain tore through her body. Blood ran down her arm and inside her elbow. She was going to faint.

"Hurry up, El." Ken and Mike's voices echoed in the hollow passage.

Eleanor's hand touched something soft: wet, cold fur. She drew back. The stench made her sick. She wanted to scream, run out of the cave. What else lay dead and rotting in the blackness? She lurched forward. The passage dipped sharply and she fell hard against the wall. Her elbow jarred. She was sweating. She pulled herself up and cracked her forehead on the ceiling.

Go on. Down. I can't.

She let Billy go, thrust her wrist into her mouth.

"El, where are you? I can't see." Billy shouted from somewhere behind her. His fingers grabbed tightly over her ankle.

"It's all right. We're nearly there."

There. Where?

She gulped warm, stale air. No smoke. She ran both hands down the cold wall. The tips of her fingers were wet. Her muscles went slack. She crouched against the wall. "We can stop for a bit. There's no smoke."

The boys huddled around her, reeking of smoke and sweat.

"I'm scared, El." Billy was shivering, huddling against her.

Scared to death. Scared of the dark, the smell. Ken's scared and Mike's scared. Scared of what might...

She put her arm across Billy's damp shoulders. "We beat that old fire," she whispered.

"This cave could go back for miles," said Mike. "We might find a river and stalagmites and stalactites."

Ken took Eleanor's arm. His voice sounded as if he had been crying. "Who told you, El? How did you know?"

"You said *she*," said Mike.

Eleanor closed her eyes. Flames danced on

the lids. She tried to replace them with images of the schoolhouse, the diary, Edward, Elizabeth.

"I think I can smell smoke," she said.

"Tell us, El. Who was she?"

She stretched back against the rock wall. "Our grandmother told me."

"What?" said Ken. "She died when you were three."

"I found her diary in the schoolhouse. From when she was a kid. She used to come here." Eleanor spat on her fingers and dabbed at the cut on her shoulder. She sniffed. Dead, stale smells.

"What's the schoolhouse?" asked Mike.

"It's that shack in our orchard," said Ken.

"It's where our grandmother did her lessons, before there was a school out here," said Eleanor. "I cleaned it up and found her diary. This cave was her place. She used to come here when she got fed up with her mum or with her teacher. She used to sit on the ledge and look at the bush. *In all its splendid colour.*

"Is that all?" said Ken. "No bushrangers and stuff like that?"

"No. Don't be stupid. Just because it was a hundred years ago doesn't mean that everyone was held up by Ned Kelly."

Billy whined, "Can I have a drink, El?"

"Wow!" said Mike. "I bet you're the first person to see that diary. It's going to make a great headline!"

Eleanor started to open the drink flask, then stopped. There was a deep rumbling from the earth above them. The wall behind her trembled and a searing blast of air struck them. Billy screamed. Eleanor threw him roughly against Ken. "That's the fire straight over us. We have to go further." She crawled on again, her fingers searching the rough stone floor, feeling each crack and pebble. The bag bounced against her knees and she swung it round onto her back.

Her eyes smarted. She rubbed them with the back of her hand.

How far before there's no air?

Billy coughed. He clutched her leg. His fingernails dug into her skin. "It's going to get us. We're goners, El!"

"Shut up!" Ken hissed as if from the end of a long tunnel.

"I can't breathe, El," Billy sobbed.

Eleanor clenched her teeth. "Just keep moving," she said over her shoulder. The tight feeling had returned to her chest. It rose and stuck in her throat.

Children Disappear. No Trace of Bodies.

Pain moved from each joint along her hand and wrist, up to her shoulder. She stayed close to the wall. Follow the wall.

You led them to the cave, you say? Twelve years old. Is that right? How does it feel, fellas, to be saved by the little lady here? One last question, exactly how did you know that the cave was there?

Stop it! Stop it! You'll go crazy.

She shook her head to clear the thoughts out. She had to concentrate, lead them on into the unknown space, tell herself there was no danger. They could survive. They would survive.

Eleanor stretched her hand out, over the floor. It was even, solid. She rested her whole weight on both hands, then brought her knees up sharply behind her wrists. She leant forward and tested the ground in front of her in a wide arc. There was a slight ridge, a crack too small to trap her hand, then it flattened out to level, solid stone. She shifted her weight forward onto her left hand. Her arm buckled under her. Rock crumbled. She fell hard and her chin hit the floor.

"What is it?" Ken grabbed her knee.

"I don't know." She caught her breath sharply. "I'm OK. The floor's gone here. Hang onto my ankles and I'll feel how far down it goes."

"Let me go," said Ken.

"I'm lighter."

Ken gripped her ankles as she leant over the edge. She ran her hands down the shallow rock grooves, over the tiny spaces left by falling stone, feeling for the dip in the floor, a space to hide. Did it fall far into the belly of the earth?

"Bit further." She wriggled forward. Her shoulders and head dropped down. Her fingers touched flat, hard stone. She spread her palms and pressed her weight onto them.

"Let go." Ken released her feet and for a moment her weight rested on her hands. Then her legs slid down the rock face and she squatted on the ledge on all fours. She coughed and reached around hesitantly. The floor continued in every direction.

"It's wide enough," she called to them. "Come on. Mike first. Then pass Billy and we'll catch him."

Mike landed feet first beside her. They put their hands up to take Bill. "Gotcha, mate," said Mike. Ken slid down after him and they sat in a line, backs pressed in to the wall.

"Are we stopping here, El?" said Billy.

"Yes," she said.

"Does it go on for miles or is there a great big hole?"

Eleanor shuddered. "I don't know. Go to sleep."

"But I'm thirsty."

She passed him the water container.

"If it comes again, we'll just lie down," Mike said. "They reckon that hot air rises and it gets to the floor last."

"Who's they?" Ken drank from the plastic bottle. "*They* reckon everything." His voice became strange and low. "Maybe *they* are out there with the dead things in the dark. Like ghosts."

"Shut up!" said Eleanor.

"There could be anything," he went on. "That rock might fall and block the entrance and we'll never..."

"SHUT UP, Ken!" Eleanor shouted this time. Billy was crying, clinging to her.

"Yeah, shut up, Ken," said Mike.

"Well, you're both thinking it too. You just don't want to admit it." He turned away from them.

Billy rolled onto the soft part of her leg. "Do you reckon that old snake got burned?" he asked.

"Maybe." She moved him slightly. He lay still for a moment and then cried out and then lay still again.

"Ssh," said Eleanor. "It's all right. I'm here."

She lay back against the wall and touched her shoulder. The blood was dry. The muscles in her legs were stiff and she wanted to stretch out and sleep but her mind was alive to every sound. Billy breathed evenly, Mike's shoe scraped on the stone as he rolled over into a more comfortable position. All around them the smell of smoke and fire lingered. She tried to think of the old house, her room painted cream and the smell under the window of piles of fresh, mown grass. But into her mind came the picture of the schoolhouse, brown slabs in the long dry grass and Mum on the verandah by the tank-stand, waving.

"Are you still awake?" Mike whispered.

"Yes." She imagined him in the dark, knees pulled up to his chin. Looking at her. What colour eyes? Hair? Skin? Suddenly it was important. What did green look like? What was red?

"Do you really think we'll be all right?" he asked.

"Do you?" Her hand was shaking. She

scooped up a palmful of dirt and let it slip through her fingers.

"Dunno," he said. "Bet you wish you'd never come here in the first place."

"No," she said. "I don't wish that. Not now." She rubbed her hands together. The dirt stung the scratches on her palms.

She slept on the cold, hard ground. Her knee stiffened under Billy's weight. Her shoulder ached.

I've lost my brother. Have you seen my brother! Open this door. Empty schoolroom. No one. He's only little. Open this door. No one. I'm responsible. Miss Wily at the blackboard. Have you seen my brother! Baby? Wrapped in swaddling clothes. Lying in a tea chest. Why don't you turn around? You've got my mother's face. I know you are Miss Wily. You must be Miss Wily...

Don't be silly. You know I can't polka. Dance with Edward. Helen, this is Edward. I mean Danny. Don't be silly, Eleanor, you know his name is Mike. His name is Edward. Edward.

I can't reach the rock. My dress is caught between my legs. Blood on my dress. Between my legs. Take the baby. The flames. The rock. I've lost your hand. Don't hold me back, Mother. I must go. Run. Run. The flames are around it. I'm afraid. I'm afraid. Can't you hear me? It's red hot. Crack! It's falling. Falling on me.

Eleanor sat up with a jolt. Sweat ran down her face. Billy breathed beside her; Ken and Mike too. The dark was cold and strange. Slowly she hoisted herself up onto the first level. Her feet slipped on the crumbling rock. Pebbles rattled behind her.

She crawled back along the passage. Her arms and legs moved automatically. There was a faint smell of smoke. The floor sloped up and turned, and she paused for a moment, breathing deeply. There was no fear any more. She leant forward to crawl again, fingers spread wide, testing slowly. They touched a smooth, round stone. She picked it up and rubbed it with her thumb. There was a slight ridge running around it. It fitted perfectly into her palm.

She pushed it down into the pocket of her shorts and edged towards the light. Out, onto the ledge. She looked up. It was still there, huge against the moonlight. Smoke drifted around it.

She climbs, pulling him up behind her. Elizabeth: Edward. Light greens. Grey-greens. Golden wattle. She takes him to the cave, smiling. Her red hair hangs loose around her shoulders.

The pale moonlight caught the black stumps. Smoke blocked out the distance. It blocked out the stars. She sat with her arms around her knees and looked down at the creek. The bank was covered with bare black trunks. There were no bushes. No birds; no frogs; no mopoke; no cicadas.

The old house, the old school would be gone, like the trees, the birds, the animals. But now she knew why her mother had come back, why Elizabeth had sat and loved the bush.

Why? Why now, when it was burnt around her? She felt as tiny as the smallest speck of ash on the rock beside her.

Nothing moved.

She buried her face in her torn hands.

13

$\mathcal{E}$leanor sat on the ledge, watching the morning light filter through the haze. A pink glow touched the burnt branches and then the tree trunks. It showed the ground, covered with ash; the remains of trees, saplings and bushes. The sun on her skin grew warmer. She stretched her legs and spat on her finger to rub her dirty knee. Beneath the black smear was a jagged scratch.

Mike came out of the cave behind her. He coughed and tugged at his hair. Soot fell around his eyes and smudged when he rubbed it. He blinked. "Have you been down to the creek, yet?"

Eleanor shook her head and stood up. It hurt. The muscles at the back of her legs pulled tight and she limped slightly. She pressed her hand into the small of her back and arched her spine.

She led the way, sliding down the bank. With every bounce, her body jarred. There were no little bushes to hold on to now. Smoke irritated her eyes and she tried to rub them. She stumbled blindly forward and fell on her knees beside the creek, in the ash and mud. She began to splash the brown water about her arms and body. It cooled her face, eased the pain in her shoulder and hands. The light caught the tiny drops that ran back over her body.

Ken and Billy ran down the bank and into the water. They leapt over the warm stones and splashed towards Mike. She watched as the water and ashes from her wet hair ran down her shoulders. Black water.

"Stop!" She hurried to the bank, shaking more black drops from her arms and hands. "We have to go. They'll be looking. We'll go that way." She pointed down the creek bed.

"Maybe we should go up." Ken faced the rock. "There could be planes out after us." He stood on one foot and pulled off his sandshoe. He tipped it up and the water drained out. He wrung it between his hands and hopped on a stone to empty the other one.

"They couldn't land in those stumpy old paddocks," said Mike. "It's probably still burning there." He turned to Billy. "You OK to walk? You've got a real shiner there."

Billy jumped from rock to rock. The weird, smoky light made his fair hair seem grey. Eleanor watched him as she walked along, her feet sinking into the ashes at the edge of the water. She was too tired to run.

She lifts him in her arms. His body bounces all the way home.

She clambered over smoking stones and fallen branches. They were too hot to touch. The fire had reached every tiny crack where the baby trees and bushes had held onto the face of the bank.

Everywhere? The orchard. The schoolhouse? It was outside the firebreak. And the diary, wrapped in soft tissue paper, tucked inside the tea chest.

"Dammit!" She cracked her knee as the branch she was treading on broke under her weight.

"We nearly got done for, El." Billy stopped and put out his hand to pull her up. His face and neck were burnt pink. He looked back at her and his eyes were the old grey-green of fallen gum leaves. "I bet they think we got cooked."

Be there. Old house, orchard, diary. Mum, on the verandah where we left you. I've brought him home, safe.

She limped after him.

Only the biggest trunks were left. They had lost most of their arms. They seemed taller now, huge and strange. Billy slowed down. He put his hand in hers. "It's like Mars, El." She nodded. There was no grass, no bushes, no little trees to push aside and let flick back.

Mum, I'm sorry I was such a pain in the neck when we first came here. And the day I said I was sick, I wasn't.

Ken and Mike stopped ahead of them. Ken prodded something with his foot. He turned it over. Tufts of brown hair clung to the charred skeleton. One outstretched paw remained, stiff.

"What is it?" asked Eleanor.

"*Was* it," said Mike. "Dunno. Something slow moving. Can't tell."

"That could'a been me," said Billy. He nudged the skull with his shoe. "Yuk! It stinks."

Eleanor started walking again.

If one of them had died and the others had to carry the body home. If they'd all died. If Mum and Dad...

She rubbed her tongue over her lips and felt the cracked skin.

Tiny flames still burned along the top of the bank. There was no wind. They weren't like the flames of the day before. They were neat, orderly like the burning leaves in the park on a crisp autumn morning.

Mum, I kept the diary for me to read. It's really yours. If it's there. If you're there.

"Flames jump firebreaks sometimes, don't they?" she asked Mike.

"Yeah," he mumbled. "But only if the fire is real strong."

Like last night.

The smoke haze shut them off from the world. Her world was the creek, Mike, Billy, Ken. The stones, stumps and the fine soot and ash.

She put her hands to her mouth and yelled,

"Cooee!" Silence. She called again, "Cooee!" It echoed off the rocks along the narrow creek bed. "Help me, you lot." The others cupped their hands. Eleanor drew in as much air as she could. Her chest was bursting. "Coo-ee!" A fly landed on the dry blood on her shoulder. She flicked it automatically. It hovered around her face.

A fly. A real, *live* fly.

A dog barked. A faint call, "Coo-ee." Ken cocked his head to one side. It came again, "Coo-ee." He slapped Mike on the back. They all jumped in the air and ran towards the sound. A red kelpie bounded out of the haze, its fur caked with mud and soot. It drew back and barked.

"Skeeter!" Mike flung himself on the dog. Suddenly, the tail began to wag. A long pink tongue licked Mike's nose and cheeks. He twisted his fingers around the dog's collar and buried his face in its hair.

Loud voices. Boots scraped on rock. Harsh cries.

"It's them!"

"They're safe!"

"It's a bloody miracle!"

Men spilled over the bank along the creek, red, green and brown shirts flecked with ash and dark with sweat, sleeves rolled up over heavy brown arms. Black, hairy arms carrying sticks, water bags, packs, a radio.

"Call back. Tell 'em we found them." They rushed forward, their faces red and gleaming.

She saw only her father. He ran out of the group and scooped his three children into his arms. He kissed her hair and pressed her tightly against his neck. She tasted sweat and smoke. The bristles on his cheek prickled her skin. Bill's elbow stuck into her chest.

Mum. Where's Mum?

She pulled back and looked at the group. Men. Only men. Tears ran down the side of her father's nose and into his open mouth. He was laughing.

She must be all right. He wouldn't laugh if...

"Where's Mum?" she asked him. He held her at arm's length. "She's at home. There are so many groups looking. She waited there in case... You're hurt." He touched her shoulder and then Bill's eye. His hands were shaking. "How did you make it? I can't believe it." He wiped his eyes with the back of his hand and left a black streak across his cheekbone.

"Is everything OK?"

"Everything's OK. It's all... How did you? Where *were* you?"

He swung Billy up onto his shoulders. "Up you go, mate." Eleanor put her hand in his. She stretched her fingers to hold it properly. Ken held his father's other hand.

Now they'll know everything. The diary. Everything.

"What about the orchard, Dad? That must've got it." Ken looked up at his father. Eleanor waited for the answer.

Outside the firebreak. It must have.

Their father shook his head. He was grinning. "It's all OK. Even your funny old schoolhouse, El. Not a scratch. I mean, burn." His face was a long way away. It was almost in the smoke. She gripped his hand and leant against his arm. She closed her eyes but then opened them and looked around for Mike. He was walking behind them. His father's hand rested in his hair. They were both talking to a man she didn't know.

They climbed slowly up the bank. She freed her hand and reached out to pull herself up. Her fingers closed over the trunk of a sapling. There were burnt streaks around the roots but above them, the green wood shone through the thin bark. She broke off a handful of leaves, crushed them and held them to her face. She stuffed them into the pocket of her shorts with the hard, round pebble from the cave.

"Get a move on, El. Your mum's waiting."

Eleanor climbed over the top of the bank. A light breeze cooled her cheeks. She could make out the tree, the huge pepper tree in the paddock. The grass all around it was burnt. The house was an eerie shadow in the distance.

Someone ran from the house, across the paddocks to the gate. She fumbled with the latch and another woman caught up with her. Eleanor ran towards them.

"Mum! Mum!"

Your eyes are red. Your hands are burnt. Bandaged. You're crying. Don't cry. I brought them home.

Her mother caught her as she fell. She kissed her face, her hair, her shoulder. She cradled her head and rocked her, the tears falling down her cheeks and onto Eleanor's matted hair.

Ken came over the side of the bank and ran to his mother. She hugged him. Then one arm reached out to take Billy.

"'s OK Mum. I like it up here." He held on to his father's hair. She pressed her face against the boy's leg and then turned back to her daughter.

"I'll take her for you," said one of the men.

"No." Eleanor shook her head.

"I can manage," said her mother. She put her arm around her daughter's waist and lifted her to her feet. Eleanor leant on her and limped across the paddock.

"It's OK, love. We're nearly there."

Who are these strange people? Cars on the drive? Go away. Don't look at me. Up the steps. Down the hall. Strange woman with Mike. Someone in the kitchen. I don't know you.

"Easy does it."

"Here's a chair."

"Gawd love ya."

An armchair in the kitchen. And a blanket. I don't need a blanket. Her mother bent down and wiped Eleanor's face with a wet towel.

"I'm all right," she whispered.

The kitchen was full of people. They talked across her, over her head. A tall man with curly black hair was frying bacon on the stove. It sizzled and spat and filled the room with its breakfast smell.

"We looked all night. You must have heard the planes. The truck went out to the dam but it couldn't get anywhere near it." Her father squatted against the cupboard as he spoke.

"How come the house didn't burn?" The hoarse voice was Ken's. He and Mike sat with their elbows on the table. Billy had climbed onto his mother's knee and she was cuddling him and whispering something that Eleanor couldn't hear.

"Bit of help from the wind. We fought it all night, when we weren't out looking for you. Some blokes are still out there getting the last of it." He stood up and his face was reflected in the mirror over the mantelpiece. As he spoke she wasn't sure if it was her father or a stranger. She blinked.

"...didn't sleep a wink. We wet the house, carried water from the creek and we blocked up all the gutters and filled them in case a spark jumped. I was sure we were goners."

"I didn't even know you were missing." The man at the stove turned round. "Struth, mate. If I'd known..." He had to be Mike's brother. He sat down astride a chair and began to eat. He leant forward and waved a fork in Mike's direction. "Are you gunna tell us, or do we have to wait all day?"

"Tell you what?"

"Where you were. What happened?" He poked a long piece of bacon into his mouth.

"How *did* you get out?"

A strange woman put a cup of tea on the arm

of Eleanor's chair. Eleanor looked around. Two more women stood, talking, near the pantry door. A man with a camera round his neck and a notepad in his hand came into the room. No one else seemed to notice these strangers.

"Drink up, love. You'll feel better," said the woman.

Eleanor started to drink the tea. It was strong and milky. She put it down.

"You kids are so damn cagey. You're not giving anything away." Mike's father leant over the table. He passed a sandwich to Eleanor. She took it but it stayed in her hand, resting on the blanket.

Go on. Ken. Mike. Sooner or later you have to. I'm too tired. It's all right.

"You all thought we got cooked." Billy slid from his mother's knee. "My throat hurts. Can I have some icecream?" He grinned at the room full of people and opened the fridge door. Ken and Mike, heads down, were drinking their tea.

"Do you want some watermelon, Ken?" asked Billy. He struggled across the room with the heavy weight. Eleanor tried to focus on the laundry door. Her school uniform, freshly washed and ironed, hung against two grey shirts. The sleeves of Ken's long one hung below Bill's.

Tell them, someone. Tell them.

Billy poured a glass of milk.

"It was real beaut," he said. "We were in El's cave and it was spooky and the dead thing was stinky and I fell in the water and nearly got drownded and Eleanor hit me."

Ken put his cup down heavily. Eyes turned to Eleanor. They all stopped drinking their tea. Flash from the camera.

"Get that thing out of here." Her father spoke roughly to the man.

"A cave," said her mother. "There aren't any caves round here."

"A cave," Mike's brother whistled.

"Were you really in a cave?" Eleanor's father looked straight at her.

She nodded. She sat back and slipped her hand into the pocket of her shorts. Her thumb touched the stone from the cave. She rubbed it and felt a tiny jagged edge. Her palm closed over it.

"How did you find it?"

"Who told you it was there?"

"How did you know, Eleanor?" Her mother shook her head in confusion.

Eleanor stood up. "You tell, Ken. I have to get something." She held onto the arm of the chair and stepped towards the door. "I have to go to the schoolhouse. She told me about the cave...her cave...not mine..." Through the gauze door she saw the twisted branches of the orange trees. She let go of the chair.

"Hang on a sec, El." Mike pushed his chair back on the linoleum. There was a splash of white paint on the black doorknob. She reached out to turn it. Pain cut from her shoulder across her back. Then her legs buckled underneath her.

When she opened her eyes it was dark. Her mother sat by the window. She came to sit on the bed. "Are you awake?" she whispered. She smoothed the sheet. "You've been asleep for hours. I've been watching you."

Eleanor tried to sit up. Her arm felt strange. There was a white bandage across her shoulder and the room smelt like a hospital.

"I bathed you like a baby. You never woke up." Her mother reached out and stroked her hair. Her other hand, bandaged, lay in her lap.

"Mum?"

"Yes."

"Did Ken and Mike tell you?"

"Some of it. They said they didn't know

everything. You'll have to fill in the details when you're better."

"It's in the schoolhouse. The diary, I mean. I haven't finished yet. It's in the tea chest, under the blackboard. I wrapped it in some tissue paper and put it under a petticoat."

Her mother blinked. For a minute Eleanor thought she was going to cry but she stood up. "I'll get it for you."

"It was her secret place, Mum. She really loved it."

The wrinkles round her mother's eyes quivered. Like someone else's. Eleanor tried to think. Who? She fell back on the pillow as her mother left the room.

She sat forward again to watch the torchlight on the verandah. It flashed over the posts and lit up the orchard. It moved towards the trees and then bobbed up and down against the wall of the schoolhouse. She giggled. She'd never seen her mother climb a fence. The light disappeared. Then she saw it again. Back it came, over the fence, across the yard. Her mother's feet padded along the hall. She came into the room and placed the yellow tissue parcel on the bed.

"Mum, it's yours really," said Eleanor.

"When you've finished," said her mother. "I'll be in later to tuck you in." She tiptoed out and closed the door.

14

14th November

Mother has just this minute left the
room. 'Sit quietly,' she said.

How can I? Each time I raise my head, I
catch sight of myself in the mirror. She
has tied a blue ribbon at the side of my
hair and it falls, with the curls, down over
the ruffles. I hope I am not the only one
with ruffles. I wish the dress were blue.

She washed my hair in lemon juice this
morning. We sat on the steps in the
burning sun and she brushed it a thousand times. It was tangled from washing
and I protested each time the brush
dragged my hair from my scalp. Edward
had gone for his customary swim and he
came up the track from the creek and
spied us there. He stared for a moment
and then turned and went through the
orchard to the back door. I have barely
talked to him alone since our quarrel. Will
he ask me to dance tonight? I do want us
to be friends again.

Mother hooked me into my dress. I
puffed and grew red in the face. She
scolded me and said I was making a fuss
about nothing. Then she smoothed the
ruffles and pinned a cluster of blue and
yellow wildflowers at my throat. 'There,'
she said, 'you look lovely. They will all
want to dance with you.'

They will not. Edward may, because he must. For the rest, I shall sit in the corner with one of the chaperones and eat the cakes that Mother sent.

It is so hot. There is a little trickle of perspiration running down behind my knees. Mother has gone to read the mail which came this morning. There was such a lot of it. I was not permitted to see any of it. I suspect that means that it has to do with Christmas.

We are to leave in half an hour. I have not seen Sarah and Kate for such a long time. I do not really want to see any of them.

Later. (Midnight)

I must write before I sleep. Indeed, I do not think I could sleep, even if I tried. I can barely recall the trip earlier this evening. So much has happened. One thing I do remember is that Edward and Father were silent for most of the way. Now I understand why. I suppose I was excited, despite my determination not to be, and I chattered away, pointing out the birds as they flew over us against the pink sky and the kangaroos that always graze on the block opposite our main gate. But I got no response from them (Father and Edward, I mean) and I lapsed into my own thoughts.

It would seem that our evening began from the moment we turned up the Jamiesons' drive. Lights flickered through the trees and, as we advanced, it became apparent that the source was dozens of Chinese lanterns that hung from every verandah post, from huge stakes driven into the ground and from ropes that hung suspended between the tops of the tallest trees in the garden. Sarah and Kate stood in the doorway and watched as Father swung me down. It seemed the whole world was staring as I led the way past the huge potplants at the bottom of the steps. I presented Edward.

'I am *so* pleased to meet you,' said Sarah. 'Elizabeth has been hiding you from us all summer.' He bowed to her with that same courteous manner that he showed to us all in the first few days. She took his arm so that I was left to follow them into the crowded drawing room. She stopped by the piano and took a card from a bowl under a painting of a particularly ferocious Jamieson relative. 'This is your dance-card,' she said, tying it to my wrist with a length of green satin. 'And now,' she smiled at Edward, 'you must meet Tom. You would have so much in common.'

Tom was leaning back against the window frame, a position from which he was able to survey the whole room. He put down his glass as we approached and affected a sweeping bow. 'My dear,' he said to me, 'how you have changed.' I have never liked Tom Jamieson. He smiles but one knows that the feeling is no deeper than the skin on his face. He tried to catch my eye, to hold my gaze, but I replied airily, 'What did you expect? The world does not stand still just because Mr Thomas Jamieson goes away to school.'

Edward started to write his name on my card. Sarah said to him, 'You must dance with all of us.' He blushed the colour of the pink buttonhole that Mother had picked for him. He wrote his name four times for me.

They announced a quadrille. I protested that I could not dance the quadrille but Edward took my hand and insisted that I should follow him. I felt so conspicuous. The lamps in the corner of the room turned my dress the colour of old parchment. At every turn he whispered instructions into my ear. I trod on his foot at least three times but he pretended not to care. I started to feel better when it came time for the barn dance. I am familiar with its steps. In fact, we began to have a capital time.

After that dance I sat out with Alice and watched the others swirling in a waltz. There were so many faces that were strange to me. I recognised the Stevenson sisters. Mary O'Donnell and Ethel Fleming who used to have lessons with us before her family moved to town. Alice sat with her hands folded daintily in her lap. It has been such a long time since we had a conversation together. I barely knew where to begin.

'They are perfect together,' she said. I looked up to see who she meant. Edward and Sarah swept past us. Her head was thrown back and her black ringlets hugged her white neck. They were laughing. Alice spoke again, 'It's the most beautiful dress in the room. I believe it is real crêpe de Chine.' I had not even noticed the dress. Even now I could not record one detail. 'Do you think,' asked Alice, 'that we shall be as sophisticated when we are sixteen?' I dug my broken nails tightly into the palm of my hand. I did not want to hear her words. I watched

Edward's black hair above the rest of the dancers. 'Your cousin has told me that he may go into the army. He would look splendid in uniform, don't you think?'

'I don't care what he does, what he wears or what he looks like. Unlike the rest of the population here!' I stood up. Suddenly I was too hot. I'm going to get a drink,' I said. I walked to the end of the room, past the sideboard laden with jellies and tarts, trifles and sweet syrups. The sight of them set my stomach churning. I slipped through the pantry and out the back door. A large bonfire blazed in front of the stables. I heard the loud, cheerful voices of men who were gathered around it. There was the smell of steak cooking and I saw a jug being passed among them. The light from the fire lit up my own father's face and, from where I hid in the shadows of the verandah, I watched him slapping his thigh and laughing with his companions. I wanted to be a child again, to scramble amongst them, to receive a sip of beer from their glasses, to be swung high in the air. The boards of the verandah creaked under my tread. I am not a child. I could not run to them.

I cursed my dress and all the other trappings of my sex. I took off my shoes and flung them into the middle of the lawn. I tugged the ribbon from my hair and, clutching it tightly, I ran across the grass, over the gate and into the bush. How often had Kate and I hidden there from the pursuers, Sarah and Tom. It all seemed such a long time ago. I stumbled on a concealed root and banged my toe. I cried out and leant against a tree. I wanted to beat my head and hands against its rough bark. The music drifted from the house. I wanted to run back through the bush, home, to my secret place. I couldn't drive from my mind's eye the picture of Edward: riding, walking, laughing and talking with me of things I have never spoken of before. I twisted my hair ribbon between my fingers. I was glad there was no moon.

A twig snapped in the bush. I darted behind the tree.

'Lizzie? Lizzie?' I knew it was him. I stepped out to meet him. 'I brought you these,' he said, and held out my shoes.

'I like to go barefoot,' I said.

'Lizzie, I've hunted everywhere for you.'

'Go away,' I said. 'They'll miss you inside. You will upset whoever is your next partner.'

'That's you,' he replied. 'Besides, they've gone in to supper.' He seemed smaller than he had on the dance floor. I started to forget my anger. We sat on the ground and I put on my shoes.

'I wanted to find you alone,' he said. 'I have to tell you that I have to leave.' I must have looked quite startled. 'No, not the dance. The farm. A letter came this morning. Father is worse and I am to take the train in the morning. Your father is going to take me when it is barely light.' Oh, how unfair, when he was going to stay till Christmas! I had thought Christmas would be such a long time in coming.

'I don't want to go.' He leant over and brushed a strand of my hair from my cheek. 'It has been the most wonderful holiday. I've never met anyone like you before.' He fumbled in his pocket. 'I won't be here for Christmas, so I want to give you this now.' The tissue paper fell from a tiny red box. I undid it slowly. 'May I write to you, Lizzie? I'll come back again, just see if I don't.' Inside the box was a fine chain and a perfect silver locket, round and flat, smaller than the one Mother wears. Even in the dark I could see fine tracing on it; a wild, rearing horse.

'Do you like it?' he asked. I could not answer him. 'It's how I remembered you from last time.' He leant over and kissed my cheek. My face burned. Am I a wild, free person? Sometimes I am so bound... so confused... I lifted my hair and he fastened the locket around my neck. Then I gave him the creased blue ribbon and he pushed it down into his pocket. We began to walk back to the house.

'Supper will be almost over,' he said. He took my hand until we reached the gate. The noise and smells of the campfire drifted towards us. He slipped away to enter by the front door, I went in by the back unnoticed.

I do not remember much more. I danced again, of course, but my shoes rubbed and I felt too preoccupied to enjoy the conversation of the others. Sarah commented loudly on my missing ribbon. I refused to divulge under what circumstances it had been mislaid. At midnight Father brought the buggy round to collect us. He and Edward chattered on about their plans for tomorrow's journey. Beneath the blanket that covered our knees I felt Edward's hand brush against my fingers. I put my head back and stared at the Milky Way. I tried to concentrate on one tiny star but it quickly blurred and melted with a million of its companions in that vast night sky.

15th November

He left this morning. The sun was not yet up and we made shadowy figures as we gathered to say goodbye at the top of the drive. He kissed Mother, and I thought for a moment he would do the same to me, in front of them all. Instead, he took my hand and thanked me loudly for being his guide and companion. I held the horses while Father loaded the luggage. Edward bent and whispered to me, 'I meant everything I said last night. I *will* come back.' I smiled and nodded, and then they were gone.

Mother sighed and said she was returning to bed. Once in my room I found I could not sleep. The only place I wanted to be was here, in my own place, high above the bush. I put on my walking shoes and ran down to the creek. I was trying to run from everything but all around me were the places where we had ridden, walked and picnicked. The locket beneath my blouse reminded me of what had passed between us. I took it out and the sun glinted on it. The laughing kookaburra seemed to mock my paltry parting gift, just a creased blue ribbon. Last night it had seemed romantic. Now, with the reason of daylight, it seems·it was childish. Tomorrow he will be back in the city with his friends and whatever future his family has decided for him. Do I have a future too? Shall I always be here?

Eleanor turned the page. It was blank. She flipped through the remaining sections of the book. There was nothing else. She stared at the final lines:

Shall I always be here?

She closed her eyes and imagined Elizabeth, sitting on the rock ledge, writing those five words. Why did she stop then? What happened the next day? And the next? She closed the book and hugged it to her. And the locket?

Round, flat silver locket. Smooth as a pebble. Traced ridges on the flat surface. Could it...?

She tossed the sheet back and ran to the light switch. There were no dirty clothes on the floor. The room was bare and tidy. She tiptoed along the hall. Light showed under the lounge door. In the kitchen the sink flowed over with unwashed plates. She squatted on the floor of the laundry and sorted through the pile of dirty washing. Each pair of overalls, each shirt and sock smelt like the fire. She tossed aside her blood-stained T-shirt. Her knees pressed into the cold cement floor.

"Eleanor, I thought you were in bed." Her mother bent over her. "What are you looking for?"

"My shorts. They aren't in my room."

"They're here somewhere." She threw the overalls into the heavy cement tubs. "What do you want them for?"

Eleanor yanked the shorts out from under a towel. She felt in the pocket. "It's not here. I had it before."

"Had what?"

"A stone, but it's not a stone. At least, I don't think..." Eleanor shook the pile of washing. She crawled under the tubs and ran her hand along the wall underneath the washing machine. She picked up a small black object and scratched it with a broken fingernail. The hard surface cracked. Light glanced off a shiny streak. "I'm not sure. I found it last night. I think it was Grandma's. From Edward."

"From Edward?"

Eleanor leant over the tubs and turned on the tap. Nothing happened.

"There's no water till tomorrow," said her mother. "Spit on it." Eleanor rubbed hard at the object.

"Edward, did you say?"

"Yes. He's in the diary. When she was about thirteen."

Her mother frowned. "Edward. The name rings a bell. Was he a cousin or something? I think there's a photo."

Eleanor followed her mother into the bedroom. They lifted the bottom drawer from the dressing-table and put it in front of them on the floor.

"The man I'm thinking of is a soldier in uniform," said her mother. "It should be with those other old photos I got when she died." She picked up the manilla folder marked "School Reports" and put it on the bed. Eleanor sifted through a handful of black-and-white snaps with neat borders: Eleanor squinting into the sun, minus a front tooth; Dad in white cricket trousers; Mum in a black flowing gown on graduation day. She put them aside next to a pile of yellowed newspaper clippings.

"This is the family taken before Harry went to the war," said her mother. She pointed to the slim woman at the back. "She'd have been married by then."

"Is this it?" Eleanor held out a photograph mounted on cardboard. A young man stood at ease with his cap tucked under his arm. He was smiling. His eyes were dark and deeply set. He had a long nose and full soft lips. She flipped the photograph over. In navy-blue ink, browning slightly where the pen had pressed heavily, was written:

To Elizabeth,
All my love,
Edward.
South Africa, 1900.

Underneath, in the same handwriting as the diary, was written in black:

VALE EDWARD JAMES WALTERS
(1880-1901)

Eleanor gripped the round, hard shape. It must be the locket. It *had* to be.

"Was she fond of this Edward?" Her mother reached out and took the photograph. Eleanor nodded. Her bottom lip trembled. Her tears blurred the edges of Edward's dark hair, his heavy serge uniform.

"Let me read it now." Her mother held Eleanor's hand and looked at the young man's face. Softly, almost whispering, she said, "Oh, Mum." Eleanor looked at her, saw her eyes fill with tears. Her huge brown eyes with tiny lines around the edges. Eyes like the eyes on the pillow when Eleanor was three.

Eleanor looked into them for a moment then buried her face in her mother's shoulder. Her body shook with sobs.

Did he come back to see her? The girl in the white, swirling dress. Wild, free spirit. She runs to the cave, scrambles towards the rock, lies old, wrinkled in bed. Her long white hair on the pillow — wild, free hair. She wants to say goodbye. She wants you specially. Say goodbye. Bye to Grandma. Byee...

15

"What happened?" Mike slapped Ken on the back but spoke to Eleanor. "You weren't on the bus. I thought you were wagging."

"We slept in." She grinned. He looked different. His hair lay flat, slicked down with Brylcreem. There were yellow iodine patches on both his knees.

Billy ran off to the Infants' School gate. Eleanor, Mike and Ken walked in through the gate marked "Boys". Kids came towards them from all directions.

"Hey, there they are!"

"They did come! Told you they would!"

Big kids. She recognised the boy who gave the cricket report on Mondays and the one from OA who got out of class two minutes early to ring the bell. Danny Stewart shot around the side of the main building. He stopped when he saw them and leant back against the corner, half-hidden by the scarlet bottlebrush.

Her left arm in its sling felt heavy and awkward.

"You'll need it," Mum had said. "They'll be all round you today. It's not healed properly yet. It needs support." She'd tied the knot firmly. "You'll be heroes today."

"Get a load of this."

"You're famous!" Mike shoved the newspaper at her. She read the headline: "HEROINE ELLIE, TWELVE, LEADS KIDS FROM BUSH INFERNO." Below was her photograph. She was wrapped in a blanket, curled up in an armchair in the kitchen. Strange people stood around her. She gazed blankly away from the camera. "On Sunday night..." she read. A scrawny boy with thick glasses pulled at her pinafore. "My dad was out looking for you."

"Did you nearly get burnt?"

"They said there was no hope."

"We heard yous were dead on Sunday night."

"Yeah, we planned your funeral already."

She felt hemmed in. The boy tugged again. His nose was covered with huge orange freckles. "My dad said you looked like ghosts when you came out of the fire."

She broke away from the group and headed for the girls' playground.

"Fire-heroine-Ellie," sang Danny Stewart. She wanted to reach out and slap him but her shoulder hurt. Instead she concentrated on the blue-black asphalt and strode towards the verandahs.

"Stand at ease. Eyes to the front. All of you."

Eleanor put her right hand behind her back. The heat from the tar warmed her bare legs. She flexed her stiff shoulders and glanced back at Ken and Mike in the first year row. Helen moved along the line and pushed in next to her.

Mr Grant, the Headmaster, began. "It is with a great deal of pleasure that I welcome back here today four of our pupils who have recently had a miraculous escape."

"Did you break your arm?" whispered Helen.

"... No doubt you are all aware of the terrible circumstances. The news has been widely reported in the press and on the wireless. I am referring to the following pupils: Mike Turner, whom you all know, and the three Wheelers who were new to the school this term."

A fly landed on Eleanor's lip. She tossed her head.

"... The four of them were trapped in the huge fire out on the Western Highway on Sunday night. There can be no doubt that their lives were in serious danger. I have been reliably informed that they owe their lives to some very quick thinking on the part of Eleanor Wheeler. At a time of great danger she remained clear-headed and led the group to safety. She is a remarkably brave girl. Let's show all of them that we are glad to see them back with us." He began to clap. The whole school joined in.

Eleanor stared down at the tiny ants which crawled out of a crack in the bitumen. In single file they advanced past a dead brown leaf. The leader stopped at a bunch of withering pink peppercorns. The rest broke ranks and swarmed around it.

"A very warm welcome back to you all."

"Fire-heroine-Ellie!" Danny Stewart hissed from behind. He slapped her on the back and her shoulder jarred.

"Pig!" She stuck her tongue out at him. She noticed Mike looking at her. He winked.

"... Pick up your cases. Seniors move off first."

"Come and sit with me today, Eleanor," Helen nudged her. They followed the line of girls out of the hot dry sun onto the cool verandah.

Kaylene waited and walked through the door with Eleanor. "Were you really out all night with Mike Turner?" she asked.

Helen opened her case and ducked behind the lid. "Come up the back at recess and tell us all about it." She pointed at the photo stuck on the inside of the bag. "Isn't John Konrads gorgeous? I can't make up my mind between him and Elvis Presley."

"That will do!" Miss Wily stepped around the desk with its bowl of fading gladioli. She picked up the blackboard pointer and tapped it against the wall. "Have you written the date yet?" She walked towards the desk where Helen and Eleanor were sitting. Her perfume drowned the smell of chalk dust and furniture polish. "We are glad to see Eleanor back, but recess is the time for chatting." She strode back to the front.

A tight wad of paper struck Eleanor's wrist and landed on her desk. She flicked it into her sling and unfolded it with her right hand. In pencil, a heart had been drawn with an arrow through it. "E.W. loves M.T. TRUE." Drops of blood dripped from the wound. Eleanor checked that Miss Wily's back was turned. She refolded the wad of paper and hurled it back across the classroom. It struck Danny Stewart's left ear. He scowled and covered his ear with his hand.

"You coming up the back?" Kaylene waited on the verandah.

"Yes, 'course she is." Helen linked arms with Eleanor. They crossed the quadrangle to the weather-shed. Behind it was a long stretch of grass with hockey goals at either end and a cricket pitch in the middle. Girls from their class sat on the spectators' mounds, their backs pressed against the paling fence.

"How did you hurt your arm?" asked Rhonda.

"Ripped it open on a stump in a gully," Eleanor replied. She squatted on the grass next to Helen.

"Did you *really* spend the night with Mike Turner in a cave?" Kaylene rolled her eyes. "Whooppee do!"

"It's no big deal, Kaylene Williams. Her brothers were there all the time, weren't they?" Helen moved closer to Eleanor to make room for Susan.

"Want a bit of my apple?" Eleanor bit hard

into the sweet, juicy fruit. Christine, Robyn, Rhonda. They'd never spoken to her before. And Susan too, who sat in the back row with Kaylene and had George and wore a bra already although everybody knew she didn't really need to. Susan held her cream bun to her lips. Red jam oozed out and her tongue slid forward to catch it. "Yeah," she said to Eleanor. "What did he do to you?" She giggled.

Eleanor crossed her ankles and balanced her sore arm on her knee. She picked at the grass with her free hand. Her grandmother's locket was cool inside her shirt.

"We went fishing on Sunday morning. Ken and Bill and me and Mike Turner. There's this dam on our place and we went there to catch yabbies. It was scorching hot so we went on to the creek for another swim. We just stayed there, mucking around till pretty late." They were all listening now. Susan licked the last drop of cream from her fingers.

"Then the fire came. I was nearly asleep in the sun and Ken just went up for a walk and saw it. We thought we had enough time to make it home. But it just went so fast. Bill couldn't keep up and he fell in the creek and we had to carry him after that. We got really puffed out, stitches and everything. You just about couldn't breathe. Anyway, I remembered this place in the rocks. A cave." She hesitated.

Secret place. Elizabeth's place.

"... and we found it. We had to go right back where the smoke couldn't get in. It really stank. It was a bit creepy and we thought there would be dead things everywhere but you couldn't see a thing. We came out in the morning and it was all burnt and we were on our way home when they found us." She shrugged.

No one spoke. She looked from one face to another. She felt she could keep talking, tell them anything.

"Wow," said Helen eventually. "It's like Enid Blyton."

"Do you reckon we could come and see it? Have a party in your cave?" Kaylene nudged Susan. "Remember that barbeque at your place?"

"No," said Eleanor. "No one's allowed there. Not till we work out all the damage."

Pushing and shoving. Shouting in her *place.*

"Ow!" A tennis ball hit her between her shoulders. She leapt up. "What do you want, Danny Stewart?"

He tucked his left arm up as if in a sling. He puffed up his chest and tiptoed along, wiggling his bottom. Behind him his mate Tony Lightfoot urged, "Go on, say it, Dan."

"My name's Ellie-smellie. I'm the biggest hero-ine in the whole-wide-west," he chanted in a high-pitched whine. Eleanor opened her mouth to speak. "And-my-brother-'ll-do-you. And-my-boy-friend-Mikey-too-oo!"

"You leave them out of this!" Eleanor swung her right hand at him. He ducked.

"Let's get him!" Helen jumped up and rushed at Danny. She lowered her head and charged, arms flying. He seized her wrists and held her at arm's length from him. She swiped at him with her foot. He shoved her aside and fell backwards against Rhonda. She kneed him in the back. He stumbled and almost fell. Kaylene kicked him hard on the shin. He hopped back towards Tony, howling and clutching his leg.

"Now git!" yelled Kaylene.

Susan picked up an apple core and a handful of stones. She tossed them at his disappearing back. "Primary School boys are just creeps," she said.

The bell rang.

"Let's all run together," suggested Kaylene, "and if any bugger gets in our way, we'll run straight over the top of him." They put Eleanor in the middle of the group, linked arms and ran hard down the spectators' mound. They charged across the field and trampled on the cricket pitch. Eleanor's legs and shoulder ached but she held her arm close to her body and kept running. They stopped at the bubblers.

Helen leant against the white bricks. She splashed cold water on her red face. "I thought you were a stuck-up snob," she said. "You never used to talk to anyone."

"No one talked to me," said Eleanor.

They walked to Assembly together. "When we have the dance," said Helen, "you can stay at my place for the night. My dad calls me Nellie sometimes. That's like Eleanor. He's putting up the aerial this Sunday. Then you can come and watch Mickey Mouse Club."

Eleanor scratched her neck where the sling was rubbing. "You could come to our place too. There's another good place I've got. I'm going to fix it up."

At Mike's stop Ken said, "I'm off to play cricket. Mike's mum'll bring me home at teatime."

"You can come too. Billy'll tell your mother," said Mike.

Eleanor shook her head. "I've got something to do at home. Another time." She grinned and waved to them as they jumped down from the step and headed off between the trees.

Eleanor sat on the back step and finished her peanut-butter sandwich. She reached inside her blouse and pulled out the locket. The sun glinted on the silver. She pressed it against her warm cheek. She stood up and went across to where the wheelbarrow lay upside down against the roots of the old pepper tree. She lifted it upright and pushed it to the workshop on the corner of the verandah.

One-handed cricket. They'd make me field.
No way.

She climbed on a trestle and took down the big claw hammer, a bottle of nails and some timber off-cuts. She loaded them onto the barrow. On top she balanced the saw, ruler and a thick lead pencil.

The rusty front wheel dug into the ruts on the track to the schoolhouse. She pushed the handle with her hip and then went round the front to tug the wheel free. Specks of ash flew up around her legs. They settled on her feet and in the tiny hairs above her ankles. She yanked and kicked the wheelbarrow through the orchard.

She rubbed the smoky glass with the back of her hand. The first piece of wood fitted neatly over the hole under the window. Her knee wedged it in place while she hammered the nails. With each blow dust flew out of the cracks in the slabs and settled on her arms and in her hair.

What about the spider? Did it ever exist?

She looked around the walls. Nothing moved. She measured and marked another piece of timber, balancing it over the step to saw. A red and black butterfly settled on the verandah post. She went back inside and banged two nails into the wood over a gap beside the door. The first nail bent.

"Damn!" Her voice echoed in the empty room. She bashed the head sideways into the soft wood and tried again.

When she finished, she straightened her back and leant over one of the desks. "Elizabeth" she traced in the fine ash. Then "Eleanor". She drew a line underneath them. "Helen" she wrote.

Eleanor and Helen sleep in the schoolhouse. Drink lemonade and tell stories till after midnight. Sit on cushions. Eat off a packing case. Read with the light from the torch. Pee out behind the old wattle trees.

"Eleanor!"

She jumped up. Ken and Mike were coming across the orchard.

"What'cha doing with all this stuff?" asked Ken.

"Fixing it up."

"Yuk! It's all smoky."

Mike peered inside the door. "You making your own place?"

Eleanor nodded.

"Want a hand?" he asked.

"Come on, Turner," said Ken. He turned to Eleanor. "Mum and Dad said we can have a party in the woolshed. We're going to check it out. This dump's too small." He pulled a splinter off the door frame. "And it's full of bugs." He swung off the verandah onto the ground. Mike didn't move.

"You stay if you like," said Ken to Mike. "I'm going up to the shed."

"Coming." Mike shrugged at Eleanor. "You coming to the dance on Friday?" He didn't wait for an answer. "See you." He jumped off the top step and raced after Ken. He caught up with him at the last orange tree. Mike put his hand on Ken's shoulder and vaulted into the air. He gripped the lowest branch, kicked his feet forward and landed on the fence rail.

"Bloody show-off!" said Ken. He climbed over the fence and turned to yell back at Eleanor. "Hey, guess what? Harry's coming back. We're not moving, though. I heard Mum say, 'Never. Not over my dead body.' She's gunna tell you tonight."

Eleanor watched them race towards the woolshed. She walked around the room, running her hands along the rough, splintery walls. She got to the tea chest, bent down and lifted out the faded petticoat. The waistband was torn. She held it against herself but it hung shapeless over her bare legs. She hooked it on a nail next to the window.

A corner of yellow tissue poked out from the purple dress. Eleanor touched it, felt something hard. A book? The diary? But that was inside, in the bottom drawer with the reports and the photographs. She knelt down and unwrapped a flat box. In it was a green leather book; a pen tied to its spine with gold ribbon. She opened it and read on the inside cover:

To
Eleanor Elizabeth Wheeler,
A special present for a
new start,
With all my love,
Mum,
Summer 1960.

She gripped the book and ran to the door. No one was in sight. She stared at the brown orchard grass and then at the clean white page. She knelt down in the last patch of sunlight on the step. The diary lay open on her lap. From down at the creek she heard the currawongs, rich warbling sounds drifting up out of the blackened bush. She pressed her back against the verandah post and sucked the end of the pen.

She began writing.